Stories Gogo told me

PENGUIN BOOKS

Published by the Penguin Group
Penguin Books (South Africa) (Pty) Ltd,
24 Sturdee Avenue, Rosebank, Johannesburg 2196, South Africa

Penguin Books Ltd, 80 Strand, London WC2R 0RL, England
Penguin Group (USA) Inc, 375 Hudson Street, New York, New York 10014, USA
Penguin Group (Canada), 90 Eglinton Avenue East, Suite 700, Toronto, Ontario, M4P
2Y3, Canada (a division of Pearson Penguin Canada Inc.)
Penguin Ireland, 25 St Stephen's Green, Dublin 2, Ireland
(a division of Penguin Books Ltd)
Penguin Group (Australia), 250 Camberwell Road, Camberwell, Victoria 3124, Australia
(a division of Pearson Australia Group Pty Ltd)
Penguin Books India Pvt Ltd, 11 Community Centre, Panchsheel Park, New Delhi –
110 017, India
Penguin Group (NZ), 67 Apollo Drive, Mairangi Bay, Auckland 1310, New Zealand
(a division of Pearson New Zealand Ltd)

Penguin Books (South Africa) (Pty) Ltd, Registered Offices:
24 Sturdee Avenue, Rosebank, Johannesburg 2196, South Africa

www.penguinbooks.co.za

First published by Penguin Books (South Africa) (Pty) Ltd 2007

Copyright © Lisa Grainger 2007
Foreword © Iman
Illustrations © Penguin Books (Pty) Ltd and Celia von Poncet

Typeset by Mckore Graphics
Cover and layout design: Celia von Poncet
Printed and bound by: Interpak Books, Pietermaritzburg

ISBN 978-0-143-02528-3

Stories
Gogo
told me

Lisa Grainger

Foreword by Iman

With illustrations by
Celia von Poncet

To my mother, Annie,
great friend and storyteller

Contents

African Stories á Gogo

I was born in Mogadishu, Somalia, which a long time ago was known as the Horn of Africa because of the way it proudly protrudes from the rest of the continent. I spent most of my childhood growing up in the capital city, Mogadishu, but during my summer holidays I would visit my aunts in the dry, arid semi-desert land of Galkayo in the north or my uncle in the lush vegetation of Biadoa in the south.

The stories from these two parts of my childhood were a world apart and they were totally influenced by their geographic opposites: roughness and delicacy, beauty and grit. Tribes on our continent have storytelling in their blood, yet each one is different from the other. Storytelling in Africa, like most of our traditions, are ways to be connected to spirit and soul.

Storytelling provides children with flights of imagination, a code of morals, and the adults with an extensive oral tradition. It's like mothering ... it's creative nurturing.

In my homeland it was not only mothers or women who were the storytellers. In our house my father was the designated storyteller.

The security I felt in my father's lap at the bewitching storytelling hour of early evening in Africa has sustained me throughout my adult life. Those stories, like stars, illuminated my path when I was lost. They have given me warmth when I felt cold and connected me to my motherland when I moved to the West.

Miraculously, through the Gogos' storytelling, these stories continue to exist and are passed on. As with modern tribes today, this book is a reminder of the power of wonder and a symbol that personifies a group unity in our families, communities and the world at large. Share it and pass it on.

IMAN

'It is in Africa's old voices that Man's richest stories lie.'

In almost every village in Africa lives a storyteller. Telling stories is not her official job. By day she may be a Gogo (or granny), a teacher, a farmer or a seamstress. But at night, round the fire, she will sit, surrounded by young children, old friends, neighbours and travellers, and will tell of how it was in the olden days, when the earth was young, when man was a hunter-gatherer, and when the animals roamed wild throughout the continent.

The stories are for old and young alike, but it is usually children who beg her to sit down after supper. 'Please, please, Gogo,' they will plead in unison. 'Sit and tell us a story.' If she isn't too busy, tending to food or family or her home, she will. Sitting on a little wooden stool under the stars, she will close her eyes, and think back to the tales her grandmother told her when she was a girl. Then slowly, by the light of the fire, her face will light up and she will begin with the words everyone loves to hear: 'Once upon a time ...'

Some storytellers I met when travelling round southern Africa with my tape-recorder were men and women in their eighties or nineties who had been telling tales in their village for more than half a century. None of the fables came from books; they were all told from memory and varied according to the tribe the storyteller belonged to. Some included songs, and listeners enthusiastically joined in, clapping and swaying and shouting. Others required the storyteller to imitate the grunts and growls of the African jungle, as she brought favourite African characters to life: the naughty hare, the wise old tortoise and the greedy baboons. Some were told to teach a moral or a lesson. And all brought howls of laughter to the village.

I hope you enjoy these stories as much as I did while travelling through villages in Zimbabwe (my birthplace), Zambia, Botswana and South Africa. The proceeds of this book, I hope, will bring some happiness to the men and women who told me the stories. A few – like the poetically named Chirikure Chirikure in Zimbabwe or Gcina Mhlophe in South Africa – are established storytellers who can support themselves. But many of the others are old and poor villagers, either bringing up AIDS orphans alone, living with leprosy or trying to survive after years of drought. But no matter how hard their lives, all of them seemed happy to sit down round the fire after a hard day to say: 'Paivapo?' (Are you listening?), knowing that they will get an enthusiastic 'Dsepfunde, Gogo. Dsepfunde!' (We're here, granny!)

So, close your eyes, think of a dark, star-studded African night filled with woodsmoke, chirruping frogs, the laugh of the hyena and the crackle of flames and try to imagine Gogo, Africa's granny, as she reaches back into her memory, and the spirits of her ancestors, to say 'Once upon a time ...'

LISA GRAINGER

Why Tortoise's shell is cracked

Told to me in Bemba by Godfrey Chanda, a subsistence farmer near Kalamazi rose farm, outside Lusaka, Zambia

Once, a long time ago, the earth was perfectly stocked with food and water. Every river ran clear and sweet. Every tree hung with fruit. Every blade of grass was green and crisp. There were treats around every riverbend and every mountain top for the animals to eat and every creature on earth was fat and happy.

There was so much food that, one day, King Lion decided to celebrate with a feast. 'Gather your favourite foods and let's meet this afternoon under the fig tree,' he announced. 'This will be the greatest of all feasts.' The jungle was a mass of moving animals as everyone hurried about, gathering their favourite titbits: marula berries for Elephant, rivergrass for Hippo, sausage tree fruit for Giraffe and soft roots for Hare.

At sunset, everyone met under the fig tree and began munching and crunching with gusto, from the tall giraffe crunching his succulent sausage fruit to the tiniest bat softly sucking its guava. By midnight, everyone had had a marvellous time – except one poor old creature: Tortoise. The slow fellow had taken so long to gather his favourite cabbage leaves that by the time he arrived, the party was over and his friends were burping and barking and heaving their fat bellies off to their beds.

Tortoise was very upset. As he sadly trundled home, he passed some birds in a tree. 'What's wrong, Tortoise?' they asked, chirruping and cheeping. 'Why are you crying?'

'The animals had a feast today, and I am so slow I missed it,' wept the tortoise. 'I was looking forward to a chat over a bit of wild cabbage, but when I arrived, no one wanted a nibble or a natter.'

The birds felt very sorry for Tortoise. His face was so tear-stained and his mouth looked so downturned that there was only one thing they could do: hold their own party the next day. 'And you will be our guest of honour, Tortoise,' they smiled. Tortoise was very excited. He had never been to a birds' party before. Then his face went glum again. 'Birds usually have their parties up in the sky,' he complained gloomily, 'and I am a big heavy tortoise. How I am I going to get up there?'

He had a point. How were they going to fly him up to their favourite cloud, the birds asked. Then Kingfisher piped up. 'I've got an idea,' he chirruped cheekily. 'What if we birds each donated a feather to Tortoise, and the bees gave some wax to stick them on? Wouldn't he then be able to fly up to the sky?'

The birds all agreed that was a marvellous idea and one by one they flew down to give the shelled creature a feather. First came King Eagle with a big glossy one, then Vulture with a speckled one, followed by Hawk, then Bulbul, then Sparrow, then Weaver, then Ibis, and Stork, and flocks and flocks of tiny, rainbow-shaded birds. Before long, in front of Tortoise's scaly head, lay a magnificent array of green, blue, black, white, yellow, red, striped, speckled and dotted feathers – gifts from the smallest finch to the largest ostrich.

Tortoise had never had so many gifts before, and once his friends, the bees had kindly spread their yellow wax onto his shell and his legs, and buzzed about sticking the feathers down, a great grin spread across his face. With a run, a jump and a flap of his little legs, Tortoise was soon airborne, and whizzing up high towards the birds' cloud in the sky.

When he reached the cloud, he couldn't believe the feast the birds had assembled. There were green grasshoppers and geckoes. Plates of red ladybirds and wriggly worms. Crawly caterpillars and traily snails. And trays and trays of leaves, and cabbages, and grass, and fruit. What a feast!

Tortoise's mouth started drooling. But before anyone was allowed to eat, King Eagle asked them all to introduce themselves to their new guest. 'I am Kingfisher,' said the kingfisher, flying forward and flashing his emerald wings. 'I am Warbler,' sang the sweet-voiced warbler. 'I am Egret,' fluttered the dainty white egret. Then the sparrow stepped forward. 'And who exactly are you?' he asked Tortoise.

Tortoise looked confused. 'Well, I have everybody's feathers on my back, so I suppose I am Everybody,' he said. Then King Eagle stepped forward. 'Now the introductions are over, I open the feast. It is for everybody, so everybody tuck in.'

The birds looked confused. Was it for them? Or was it for Everybody the tortoise? Politely they held back, and watched as their guest tucked into the wonderful feast. Head down, eyes to the floor, Tortoise munched and crunched, without looking up once. First he gobbled all of the birds' favourite foods, which he didn't normally eat: the grasshoppers, then the geckoes, then the ladybirds and wriggly worms. Then he crunched his way through the caterpillars and snails. And once he had devoured that, he started munching on the all of his own favourites: piles and piles of lovely lush leaves.

The birds weren't pleased with Tortoise's rudeness – especially when he casually announced he was going. 'At least you could say thank you,' muttered grizzly Owl. 'Or offered to share a worm, which we know you don't even like,' muttered Crow. 'Or halved a caterpillar,' grunted Egret. But, no. Tortoise was selfish. He was used to living alone, and not sharing, and so, when he finished his feast, he licked his lips and turned around to fly home off the edge of the cloud.

The birds were furious. How dare Tortoise eat all their food and not say thank you? If he was going to be so rude, they decided, they were all going to take their feathers back from him. So, in a great flock, the birds all swooped on Tortoise, each pecking their feather off his back. And slowly, Tortoise felt himself sinking deeper and deeper into the cloud.

'Help!' he cried, as he sunk into the whiteness. 'Help, someone!' But not a single bird came. 'If you think you are Everybody, then help yourself!' they squawked, flying away crossly to their nests.

Of course, without feathers, the heavy Tortoise fell to the earth with a tremendous thud. The landing was sore and very undignified. But even worse than that – it had ruined his shell. His once beautiful, glossy, glamorous outer layer was gone, and in its place was a shattered mess of a hundred tiny squares.

Today, if you look at a tortoise, its shell is still cracked. The gods left it that way as a reminder to all creatures – of what happens when you take your friends for granted. Love them and you will fly high. Forget them and you will fall. Just like Tortoise did.

Why Rabbit's tail is short

Told to me in Ndebele by Lindani Nlotshwa in Bulawayo, Zimbabwe, and in Bemba by Godfrey Chanda in Zambia

Once upon a time, long back, when animals could talk and Hare had a long tail, there was a terrible drought. The leaves shrivelled up. The puddles turned to dust. And the waterholes slowly dried and cracked, leaving the animals with nothing to drink. Even when they prayed to the great Rain God, the air remained empty and dry, without a single cloud in the sky.

King Elephant became desperate. He hadn't had a drink for two days, or a mud bath for a month. So he decided to call a meeting. 'Cheetah!' he trumpeted to his chief messenger, who was lying in the shade, trying to keep cool. 'Go and call all the animals. We must meet.'

Being the fastest animal on earth, it didn't take Cheetah too long to relay the king's message. He ran from river to rock, from grassland to grotto, and from treetop to mountain top until, by the end of the day, the animals had all gathered under the great baobab tree.

When they had all quietened down, the Elephant began. 'Subjects,' he trumpeted, swaying his body importantly from side to side. 'We are in grave danger. Our waterholes are almost dry, and soon we will die of thirst. Either we must move to a wetter area, or we must make a plan. I've given up on my ideas. So if anyone else has one, would he please step forward.'

At first no one said anything. Then Impala and Gemsbok, the shy little buck of the bush, started to whisper to each other. 'Speak up, speak up!' thundered Elephant. 'If you've got something to say, trumpet it out, trumpet it out!'

'Well, Your Majesty,' whispered Impala, his skinny front legs shaking with nerves, 'what about digging a well? If all of us helped, it wouldn't take long. We could take it in turns to guard it, day and night. And then we might have water for ever.'

The animals couldn't quite believe that such a big idea had come from such a small creature. 'You are quite brilliant!' said the king proudly. 'Tomorrow, as you have suggested, we will start digging. And you will be the first to be rewarded with the sweet water when the well is finished.'

The next day, as agreed, all the animals gathered in a sandy spot by the riverbank to dig. Every animal, that is, but lazy Hare. 'Me?' Hare said, flicking his beautiful, long, fluffy tail. 'Why should I want to drink from your silly well? I have juicy roots to gnaw in my burrow, and an underground spring to sip from. Thanks, but I'd rather have a snooze here in the shade.'

Digging a well took a whole day, but at the end of it, the animals heard a wonderful sound coming from the bottom. 'Water!' Python gurgled, as he slowly floated up on a bubbling pool of liquid. Excitedly, the bucket was passed to the front, and as promised, when the first bucket was drawn Impala was given the first sip. The water was not only cold. It was sweet, pure and clear – the nicest water anyone had ever tasted.

Over the next weeks, as the earth became drier and drier, the animals congratulated themselves on their magnificent well. Only Hare wasn't happy. The spring had disappeared from its underground spot, and the roots had shrivelled and dried.

But whenever he tried to get to the well, some fierce creature was guarding it. And the animals all said the same thing. 'Sorry, Hare, but you didn't help us to dig, so you can't drink either. Goodbye.'

Hare was becoming very cross. He couldn't be bothered to dig his own well. He didn't fancy pleading with the king for water. So there was only one thing left, he decided to steal it.

That night, he crept quietly behind the well, and with just a little hop, he was at the bottom, sipping lovely cool, sweet water. 'Hahaha, you are a clever chap!' he laughed to himself, as he inched his way back up. But Hare was not quite as clever as he thought. The watchful guard had spotted him leaping in, and immediately called the animals. Just as Hare got to the top, he was caught. Then a great roar erupted into the night. 'Hahaha,' laughed Hyena. 'Hissssssshissss,' hissed Python. 'Snortttttt, snortttt,' huffed Hippo. 'We have caught the water thief!'

Even King Elephant had a triumphant trumpet, before quietening the animals for Hare's formal dressing down. 'Hare, you are a disgrace to the animal kingdom,' he harrumphed haughtily. 'Not only have you been lazy, and failed to help us dig the well, but you have stolen water that doesn't belong to you. You must be punished.'

Hare's long tail started to quiver with terror. 'King, oh, King,' he said. 'I know I have done wrong. But whatever you do, please don't swing me by my ears and tail and throw me onto the sand. That's what every hare dreads.'

Elephant surveyed him with a frown. 'If that is what hares dread, then that is what we must do,' he said. He called for the sharp-toothed dog to hold Hare's long tail and Hyena to hold the rabbit's ears. Then, as the animals roared and snorted, they swung Hare into the air and thumped him onto a pile of yellow sand. When he lay there quite still, there was a rumbling cheer. 'Justice has been done!' the animals yelled. 'Let's go and celebrate.'

But as usual, Hare had tricked his fellow creatures. No sooner had they turned their backs than he leapt up, gave a gleeful shout and then hopped for his life. 'Silly animals,' he giggled as he bounced this way and that. 'Don't they know how soft sand is? It's like a pillow to us hares!'

The animals hated being tricked once. But being tricked twice was really out of order. 'After him!' trumpeted Elephant furiously, as the paths pounded with creatures in pursuit. Lion was at the front, but before he could even yell 'Burrow!' Hare was down one, his long tail slinking swiftly down the hole. Sadly, it didn't slink down quite fast enough, and with a pounce Lion caught it and bit it off sharply between his teeth.

Hare howled and cried, and hopped up and down with agony, but it was too late. His beautiful long tail was gone – lopped off by Lion. Look at it today, and see how stumpy it is – a constant reminder that Hare had cheated – and lost.

Why lightning strikes

Told to me in Tonga by Mafuta Siabwanda in Bulawayo, Zimbabwe

Once upon a time there lived a woman called Lefu, who was loved by everyone in her village. Lefu was poor, but she was generous, kind and always smiling, especially when she was with her daughter Minni. She loved Minni. Every day, when they'd take their clay pots to get water from the river, she would sing a song to thank the god Mulungu for such a happy life. 'Thank you Mulungu for food, sun and water, and thank you for giving me my precious daughter,' she sang sweetly, as her friends the birds whistled along.

In the same village lived three women, who had plenty of earthly riches, but were terribly mean. They never shared anything – their food, their conversation, or their song – preferring, rather, to sit in their huts, counting their pieces of cloth, admiring their goats, stuffing their fat bodies with porridge, and complaining.

Complaining was their favourite hobby, particularly if it was about Lefu. 'Why should she be loved more than us by the rest of the village?' they would gripe through their mean mouths. 'We are much richer than she is. All she has is that silly smile on her face.'

One day their jealousy became so great that they could not stand Lefu's smile any longer. They came up with a horrible trick to play on her. At the hottest part of the day, when Lefu and Minni were gathering water at the river, the three women appeared from behind a tree. 'Hello, Lefu,' said the first woman, a fake smile lighting up her normally mean face. 'The sun is so hot today that all three of us have thrown our children in the river. They are so happy and cool now. Why don't you throw Minni in? The poor girl looks boiling!'

Lefu was a bit apprehensive, but her daughter looked so hot, and the women seemed so unusually helpful, she agreed. But the minute that Minni's body splashed into the water, the three women began to cackle through their yellow, cracked teeth. 'You love making people happy, Lefu,' hooted one noisily, 'and today you will have made Crocodile's day. He doesn't usually get plump young girls for his dinner.' Before Lefu could even cry out, Crocodile had risen from the river bed, snapped up Minni and vanished under the water.

Lefu was distraught, and ran back to the village crying out for the village warriors to come and help her. They took their spears to hunt the great beast. But it was too late – Crocodile had vanished, with Minni in his belly. 'Oh God Mulungu, who gives me food and water,' wept Lefu under a tree by the riverbank. 'Please help me to get back my precious daughter.'

Leopard, who had been lying eating an antelope on a branch above Lefu's head, took pity on the weeping woman who usually sang so sweetly. 'Lefu, climb up here,' he purred softly, 'and I will help you find your way to the great god Mulungu. It is a long journey into the sky, but if you climb my tree, at least you'll be nearer the clouds.'

So, with Leopard's help, Lefu climbed the tree to the tips of its strong branches. When she got to the top, her friends the birds offered her further assistance. 'Come with us, sweet Lefu,' they sang, lifting the woman onto their wings and flying her into the sky. When they reached the stars, the great fishes of the sky, the Mazomba, took over. They lifted Lefu from the birds, and swam her through the stars in the great Lake Sky. Eventually she reached the village where the great god Mulungu lived.

When Mulungu heard her sweet voice, the god immediately recognised the sweet woman who sang praises to him every day, and took pity on her. At once he ordered Crocodile to come and see him.

'I know Minni was your supper, Crocodile,' said Mulungu, 'but Lefu needs her beloved daughter back. I promise that, if you obey me, I will see that you have plenty of food to make up for that snack of little Minni.'

This sounded like a good deal to Crocodile. So he belched, and his tummy squelched, and out of his long, toothy mouth popped a slightly wet, and squashed-looking, Minni. 'Oh thank you, Mulungu,' cried Lefu happily, hugging her daughter and drying off Crocodile's saliva. Then the two of them set off home again – this time with their new friend the Crocodile, and a great bundle of gifts from the god for their journey.

When they got home, the villagers prepared a celebratory feast and Lefu sat round the fire and told them of her great adventure in the sky. When she showed them Mulungu's gifts: cloth and food and gold, the villagers were delighted for the sweet Lefu – except, of course, for the three greedy old women. 'Why should that silly, smiley Lefu have those gifts?' they complained. 'If she can trick Mulungu into giving her all that, surely we could have even more?'

So the next day, the three women threw their own three children into the river, and, huffing and puffing, hauled their fat bodies up the tree where Leopard lived to make the long journey to the great god Mulungu. The trip took them much longer than Lefu's, as none of the animals wanted to help such miserable, miserly old women. But after a few days of beating and prodding the reluctant birds and beasts, the three women arrived at the god's village.

Mulungu was not pleased. After all, gods don't like to be ordered about. They don't like their animals being maltreated. And they especially don't like lazy, malicious, mean old women coming to lie to them. At first Mulungu listened patiently to the women's sob story, of how they had mistakenly lost their beloved children in the river, and how their dear friends the animals had helped them reach the village.

But slowly his face darkened, and his voice turned to thunder. 'Old women,' he bellowed, as the rain clouds around him turned black.

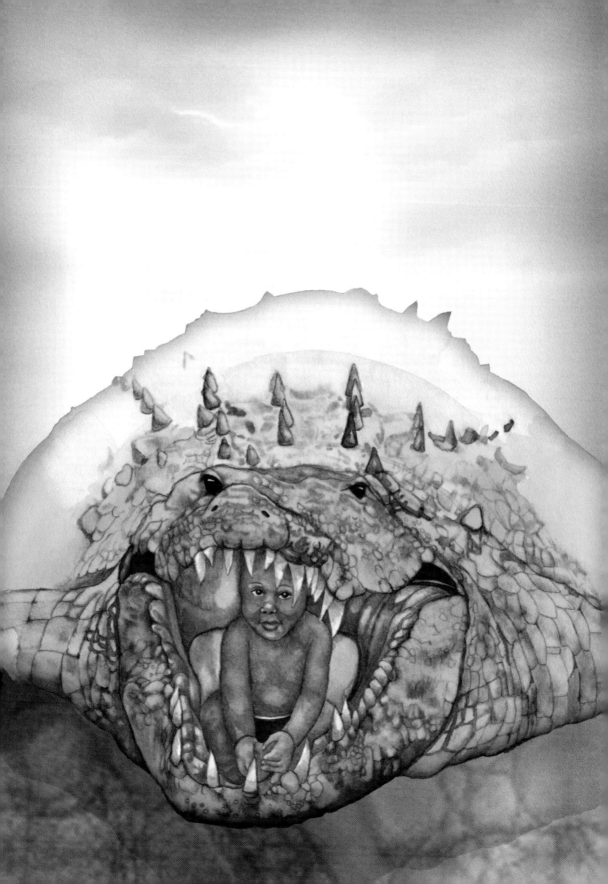

'Have you not learnt any lessons in life? You have done every bad thing a woman can do – fooling a mother into killing her daughter, lying, throwing your children into the river, and now trying to trick me into giving you things. Well, if you want things, you will get things. But it will be things that you deserve!'

The god then raised his hand furiously into the sky. As he did, the clouds blackened, the wind started to blow, and a monstrous bolt of lightning shot from his palm, striking all three women down and throwing their bodies down through the sky into the river for the hungry crocodile to eat.

The village was glad to be rid of the three wicked women, and to welcome home Minni and Lefu. But no one will ever forget that day: the time that Mulungu took the liars and sent them back to earth in lightning. Whenever there is lightning, liars look particularly nervous. For they know it is a sign that the great god Mulungu is watching for wickedness from above.

Why Hippo flings his dung

Told to me in English by Aubrey Mbewe, a game guide at Kisani Lodge in the Luangwa Valley, Zambia

When the Creator first made the earth, Hippo was a land creature. A greedy land creature. All day he would wander the riverbanks and plains, chewing and chewing and chewing. The more he chewed, the fatter he got. And the fatter he got, the more he hated the hot African sun.

'Oh great God,' he muttered miserably as he heaved his fat, hot belly down to the river for a drink. 'I wish I could cool down. How I envy those creatures that don't have to bake in the sun, but who wallow happily in the water. I wish I could join them.'

One day Hippo could take the baking sun no longer. His skin was wrinkled and cracked, his nose was sunburnt and he could hardly talk his mouth was so dry. 'Please, Creator,' he begged. 'Let me go and live in the river. I am so unhappy in the sun. I promise I will behave.'

The Creator wasn't convinced. 'Everywhere you go, Hippo, you eat everything in sight,' he said. 'On the riverbanks you eat the river plants. On the plains you eat the grass. If you lived in the water, you would undoubtedly eat all the fish too. Besides, what would the crocodiles say? It's their home too, you know. And we can't have two hungry animals living in the same water. I'm sorry, but the answer is no.'

At this news, Hippo wept and wailed. By day he heaved his fat belly around, chomping grass and drinking water. And at night, he complained by the light of the moon. 'Oh Creator, please!' he wept.

'Today my nose got sunburnt, my ears got sunburnt, and even my tummy got sunburnt. I'm so unhappy in the sun that I am prepared to make you a promise. I promise that, if you let me live in the water, I will only stay in it in the day. By night I will get out of the river and eat grass by the light of the moon. And never, ever will I touch a fish. I promise, I promise, I promise!'

The Creator, feeling sorry for the poor sunburnt Hippo, agreed – on one condition: that the fat creature never, ever ate a single fish. 'And to prove it,' the Creator said, 'every time your food passes through your body, I want you to spray it around with your tail. As your dung flies through the air, Hippo, I will personally inspect it. If I ever see a fishbone in it, I'm warning you, you will be out on the riverbank in the sun again.'

Thanking the Creator, the very happy hippo jumped straight into the water, where he still lives today. Occasionally during the day you will spot his nose and ears poking out of the water while he keeps his body cool under the water. But he always comes out at night to graze, and whenever he does you can see him keeping his promise to the Creator. Watch his tail you will see it spinning about, sending his dung flying into the sky. And occasionally you will hear him grunt 'Look, God, no fish, Look God, no fish!' just to prove his point.

Why Hare's ears are long

Told to me in Shona by Blessing Cabbage in Mabvuku, Zimbabwe

A long time ago, before Lion was king, Elephant was the ruler of all creatures on earth. He was the biggest, the strongest and the wisest animal God had ever made, so it was only natural that he should rule the kingdom.

One day King Elephant decided to call a meeting of all of the antelopes. This was unusual, because normally he invited everyone, but this time he needed to discuss something that concerned the antelopes only. So he sent out an urgent message calling all the antelopes to meet under the baobab tree.

Hare, as usual, had his ears pricked into the air, and soon he had heard the message too. He was very cross. Wasn't he smarter than anyone else? Craftier than anyone else? And faster than everyone else? If so, why was he being left out of the secret meeting?

For two days and two nights Hare sat grumpily in his burrow. 'How am I going to get to the meeting?' he pondered. Then at last he came up with an idea. 'I know!' he giggled, hopping about happily in his burrow. 'I will make myself into an antelope!'

After making sure that no one was watching him, Hare set off in great excitement. He hopped and he skipped, over logs and over the river. When at last he got to a hollow tree in the forest, he gave a leap of joy. For there was a tree trunk containing the most enormous deserted bees' nest he had ever seen. And in that nest were honeycombs full of precious golden wax.

Hare couldn't stop grinning. 'Hohoho!' he chortled happily, hopping from foot to foot with glee. 'Look what the bees have made for me!' And quickly he began stuffing his little bag full of wax, before hopping home.

When he got back to his burrow Hare wasted no time completing his plan. With his deft little fingers, he soon was shaping, smoothing and shining the wax until, in his hands, he held a pair of the most beautiful, elegant and realistic antelope horns he'd ever seen. He tried them on for size, adjusted them between his two short little ears, and wiggled his head about to make sure they stayed on. Then, with a contented sigh, he settled down for the night, dreaming of how handsome he would look as an antelope.

The next morning, Hare leapt up and excitedly tried on his new headdress, sticking it down firmly with wax on his head. After looking at himself in the waterhole, he had to congratulate himself. 'The animals are right, Mr Hare,' he said, swaggering at his reflection, 'when they say you are a handsome and clever chap. Indeed you are! Yes, you are!' And off he trotted, as antelope-like as he could, to the secret meeting.

Under the great baobab tree, the antelopes had all gathered, and were snorting and harrumphing in anticipation of the big occasion. All types of horns were mingling together. On one side stood the bighorned animals: Eland's curly and twisted, Sable's notched and arched, Waterbuck's black and straight. And on the other stood all the tiny buck, from Duiker to Impala, wiggling their little horns and snorting impatiently.

Nervously, Hare slipped in between them, lowering his head so no one would notice him. Fortunately, most of the antelope hadn't seen each other for a while – some being from the mountains and others from the valleys – so they took little notice and kept on chatting. And soon, King Elephant was trumpeting the start of the meeting.

'As you know, oh Horned Ones,' started the king, 'we are here for a secret meeting to discuss matters related only to us. I would ask you to keep whatever you hear to yourselves.' The antelopes all nodded in unison, including Hare. But as he did so, he thought he felt something wobble. 'Oh no!' he said to himself, his eyebrows shooting up in panic. 'My horns – they're slipping!'

Sure enough. While the horns had looked perfect earlier, what Hare had forgotten was that wax melts. And in the hot morning sun, his elegantly crafted horns were slowly dripping off his head. First he felt a warm drip down his nose.

Then he felt a strange, warm, melting sensation on his head. And then – embarrassment embarrassment of embarrassment – one of his horns fell right off, in full sight of all the antelopes, and yellow wax streamed down his face.

The meeting went quiet. Then everyone started grunting and stamping their feet. 'Rotten spying Hare!' snorted Eland. 'Traitor!' trumpeted Reedbuck. Together the creatures lowered their horns and stormed the wet, sticky creature, before taking it in turns to pick him up by his short little ears and toss him like a ball from antelope to antelope. When the creature was filthy, and waxy, and a bit bruised, the king trumpeted. 'I think Hare has learnt his lesson, fellow creatures,' he said, surveying the hot, waxy animal lying in a ball in the sand. 'And I trust now his new head ornaments will remind him for ever more that not everything is his business.'

Shamed, and slightly sore, Hare stood up and hopped home. When he saw a waterhole, he stopped to look at his reflection. What he saw horrified him. His horns were gone – but what had happened to his ears? He looked again, thinking his eyes were tricking him, but they hadn't. On his head were the longest ears he had ever seen – long, fluffy ears that rose from his head straight into the sky. 'Well at least I will be able to hear well,' he sighed, and hopped off home.

Hare can hear much better now, thanks to his new ears. But they haven't really helped him hear any more secrets. For every time a jungle creature sees a hare coming, it remembers to keep its mouth shut. Those big ears are a reminder that a hare is a creature which would like to know everything and will do anything – even make himself horns – to find it out.

Why Frog can no longer sing

Told to me in Ndebele by Monica Khumalo in Bulawayo, Zimbabwe

Once upon a time, the frog was the greatest singer in the animal kingdom. Its voice was sweet, and its songs clear, and animals would travel from faraway lands to hear its recitals on the banks of the river.

In a nearby village lived a great and good chief who was loved throughout the land. His cattle were fat and his villagers had rich supplies of food. Their water was cold and plentiful. And there was peace throughout their land. It was a time of great happiness.

The chief was fond of all his people, but his favourite was his youngest daughter, a sweet, kind and very beautiful young girl. One day the girl and her friend decided to go swimming. It was a hot day, and they walked through the sunny forest until they reached a cool pool. They had never been to this pool before, but it was so leafy overhead, the water was so clear and the banks so grassy that it seemed a perfect place for a swim. Soon they were splashing about, their laughter ringing in the leaves above.

It so happened that this pool was the one in which Frog lived. That day, he was sitting on his favourite lily leaf, warming up his voice for his evening singsong. 'What a lucky frog I am,' he hummed happily, 'to be king of such a cool pool. In fact I'm such a lucky king, I might even start to sing.' He opened his mouth, stretched his great green throat into the air and prepared for a sensational singsong.

Frog swam through the choppy water, until he reached the surface. Just as he put his head up, another wave came whooshing towards him. This one, too, went straight into his mouth and down into his froggy lungs. 'Crooooooaaaak!' he spluttered, as his fat body sunk for the second time. 'Crooooooaaaaak!'

Frog was extremely unhappy. Every time he tried to raise his head above the water, he got knocked back under. And every time he tried to protest, a strange croaking sound came out of his mouth. 'Croooooaak,' it went. 'Croooooooaaak!'

Tired and half-drowned, Frog swam to the bank and slowly crawled out, shaking the water from his mouth and ears. Once on solid ground, he looked round to see who had dared to dethrone him. There in the pool were two girls, splashing and singing, lurching his lily pad thrones about as they did so.

'Foolish females,' he gargled through his water-filled throat. 'Do you not know that I am King of the cool pool? You must be punished!' Slowly but surely he puffed and he huffed, until his body was almost double its size. Then, when he was as round as a ball, he opened his secret little poison sacs behind his ears, and blew and blew, until horrible clouds of green noxious gases rose above his head and wafted towards the swimming girls.

The girls' laughter soon turned to coughs. Then splutters. Then howls as the poisonous gas filled their lungs. And when they could cough or splutter no longer, they both sank beneath the surface to the bottom of the pool.

Later that afternoon, the chief began to get worried. His daughter was normally back before dark. So off he set with his faithful warrior, until he reached the cool pool. Instead of his daughter, all they found was her reed skirt and beaded necklace. And a fat frog sitting on a lily pad.

'Oh, King of the cool pool, and singer of great songs,' said the chief. 'Have you seen my precious daughter? Her skirt is here, and her necklace is here, but her smiling face has gone.' Being a cowardly fellow, Frog just shook his head and opened his mouth to sing no. But instead of sweet little froggy notes, a terrible croaking noise out of his throat. 'Naaaaaooooaaaaooooooo,' he gurgled and croaked, cringing in horror at the awful tones. The chief looked at him suspiciously. 'That sound, Terrible Toad, is a sure sign of punishment from the gods,' he said. 'It is the voice of guilt. And from now on, Man will abhor you. You will be forbidden from singing during the day, and Man will hunt you until the end of your days!'

From that day on, frogs have avoided Man, hopping off their lily pads at the mere sight of one. They are also very sorry for what they have done. Listen carefully at night and you will hear them croaking mournfully from ponds, remembering the great days when they were the kings of the cool pool.

Why Crocodile has no tongue

Told to me in English by Gcina Mhlophe,
a professional storyteller,
in Johannesburg, South Africa

Once, a long time ago, a drought came to the earth. Every day both Man and animals looked up to the sky, praying it would rain, but it never did. The fields became cracked from the fiery sun and the waterholes shrivelled up. Soon there was nothing left on the earth but red hot dust and a couple of puddles.

King Lion got very worried. Some of his subjects had not eaten for weeks. Giraffe's neck was bonier than ever. Impala had lost the spring in his step. Even the normally fat buffalo's ribs had started to show through his dusty black coat. Something had to be done.

So the king called a meeting. 'Animals,' he roared, as his subjects gathered in the shade of the great fig tree. 'I have called this meeting because, as you know, we have no food, and if we don't come up with a plan, we will all soon turn to dust. So, if anyone has an idea, would he please step forward.'

The animals all looked at each other, hoping someone else would come up with a solution. The impalas wagged their tails nervously. Wildebeest stamped their feet and snorted. Zebras hurrumphed and flicked their long black tails. And Elephant rumbled his throat importantly. But no one actually said anything.

Then a tiny nervous voice rose from the antelopes. 'Excuse me, Your Majesty,' said Waterbuck, shyly stepping forward to show off his white-ringed bottom. 'But I have an idea.'

The animals all looked up at the brown and white buck. 'Well,' roared Lion, flicking his tail impatiently, 'what is it? Step forward, step forward!'

Waterbuck, as you know, is a shy, solitary creature, which doesn't like crowds, so it took great courage for him to pipe up. 'As you know, King Lion, I usually drink by the river, and down there is a small pool of water and the last patch of green grass in the kingdom. If all of us planted pumpkins and mealies there, that might tide us over until the rains come. We might all then be saved.'

The animals all cheered. What a wonderful idea! King Lion praised Waterbuck, saying 'If Man can grow crops, why can't we?' and at once the animals made hoes and set off for the field. Every animal helped – either ploughing the land, planting seeds or watering them from the tiny pool left in the river. By sunset everyone was exhausted and set off home.

The field was a great source of pride to the creatures, and each day one of them guarded it and watered it. Everything was going well – the mealie plants rising high in the sky and the pumpkins ripening – until one terrible day, when Impala didn't return from his duty. The animals saw him go to the river, but he never come back. The next week Eland vanished. Then big Buffalo. The animals began to get worried, and soon no one wanted to guard the crops.

So once again King Lion called a meeting. 'As you know, Animals,' he growled. 'Waterbuck's plan is going extremely well. But a spell has fallen on the field. As fast as our crops grow, our guards vanish. Now no one wants to go to the field and our crops are wilting. We must decide what to do.'

Once again, the animals looked at each other nervously. And again Waterbuck piped up. 'Your Majesty,' he stuttered, looking shyly at the King under his long black eyelashes. 'Being a Waterbuck, I spend much of my time at the water. I usually love water. But I don't like guarding the water at our field. At night it has red eyes in it!'

'Red eyes?' snorted the king, as the rest of the animals started to snigger. 'How can water have eyes in it, silly Waterbuck? Are you ill? Do you need a doctor? Water doesn't have eyes!'

Waterbuck was most upset. 'You animals can laugh,' he sniffed huffily, 'but if any one of you will come with me, I will show you.'

The king felt a bit sorry for Waterbuck. After all, he had been brave enough to step forward with an idea. So the king agreed. 'All right, Waterbuck,' he said. 'I will accompany you. We will meet at the pool tonight.'

As agreed, under the light of the moon, Waterbuck met the king. The two of them hid quietly behind some reeds and watched and watched. At first nothing happened. Then, just as Waterbuck had said, the king spotted two huge round eyes in the water. 'You are right, Waterbuck, you are right!' whispered the king, looking terrified through the reeds. But, being a brave king, out he stepped and spoke to the eyes: 'Red eyes, red eyes shining bright, Come out of your water tonight!' he commanded.

To the pair's horror, out of the water slid the eyes until soon, under the light of the moon, lay the hugest crocodile anyone had ever seen.

They both trembled. 'Who, pray, are you?' said the king in a wobbly voice.

'Who am I?' bellowed the creature in a terrifying voice. 'I am Gongqongqo, King of the Crocodiles. I eat buffaloes whole – horns, hooves and all. I swallow impala as a snack. I have tortoises for my tea! You will be a mere morsel in just one snap, scrawny old lion!'

Waterbuck and Lion shook and quivered. This creature was scary – too scary for even the king to tackle. They looked at each other in terror and, tails between their legs, ran for their life without once looking back.

Back at home, the jungle was woken by the king's frightened roar. With eyes as large as pools, the normally brave king related in a little trembling voice what he and Waterbuck had met at the field: the biggest, fattest, longest, nastiest crocodile anyone had ever seen.

Impala looked terrified. 'He said he'd have me as a snack!' he cried, his little front legs shaking nervously. 'What will we do?'

Again, the animals were silent, hoping someone bigger and braver would come up with an idea. Then, from the ground, came a little old reedy voice. 'I'll get him!' it squeaked. The creatures looked down, and there on the ground stood Tortoise. 'Give me a little sharpened axe that I can hide in my shell,' the creature said, 'and I will rid you of this pest.' The animals gave a little giggle. But as no one had a better idea, the king agreed, and soon the animals were waving Tortoise and his little axe goodbye.

When Tortoise got to the field, the enormous green monster was lying sprawled in the moonlight. 'What are you doing here, you silly snack of a shelled creature?' it bellowed, spewing rotten fumes from his mouth. 'Don't you know I will eat you?'

To the beast's surprise, Tortoise agreed. 'Please, oh please eat me,' Tortoise begged. 'We are so short of food and water that it would be a pleasure to live in your mouth, great beast. Perhaps, then, I could share in your feasts.' And he strode straight up to the surprised creature's mouth and the great beast tossed him back under his great pink tongue.

It was exactly as Tortoise had planned. As soon as he had got to his feet under the creature's tongue, he pulled out his little axe. 'We'll see now, Crocodile, who will eat whom for a snack,' he giggled. And bit by bit he started to chop away at the great crocodile's tongue.

No matter how much the creature roared, or tossed its head about in pain and anger, Tortoise continued his job. Chop, chop, chop he went, until at last his job was done. The large crocodile's tongue fell out into the field, and with it Tortoise jumped out.

The animals, having heard the noise, rushed up to the field and there they found the creature lying tongueless on the ground. 'From now on, Crocodile,' said King Lion, standing by the creature's tongue, 'you must promise to leave our fields alone. Remember you are a water creature. Try and creep out again and you know what will happen.' With a scared little grunt, the injured crocodile crept back into his pool and the animals carried Tortoise home to celebrate his great victory.

Since then, crocodiles have rarely been seen in fields again. They are scared of creatures with axes. But if you do ever see one on land, sunbathing or sleeping with its mouth open, take a look. It won't have a tongue. Thanks to the bravery of the terrific Mr Tortoise.

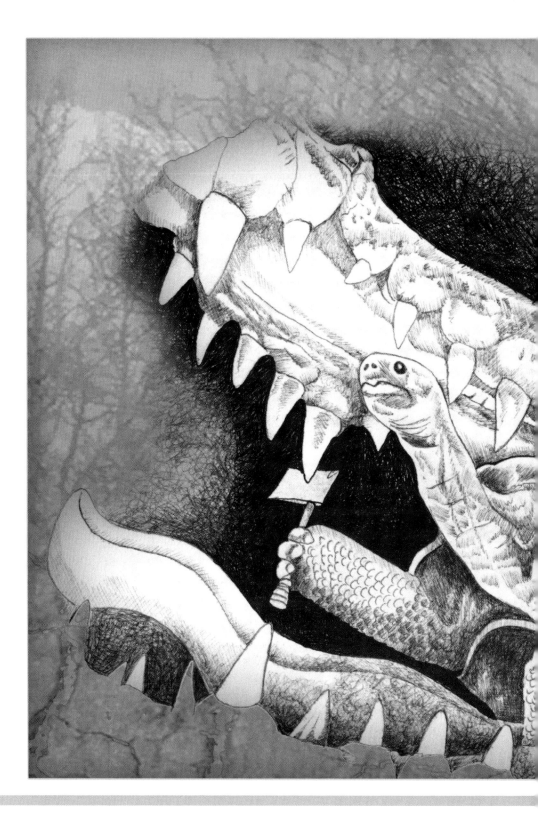

When the earth was young

This is a story of how the earth became like it is.
It is not really a traditional story, just an
explanation of why things are like they are.
Told to me in San by Nxexao Kgimxow in
Botswana

Today earth is like a three-storey house. On the top floor live the gods, the sun, the moon and the stars. On the middle floor lives Man, the animals, the rivers and the plants. And on the bottom live the dead, and the gods who are taking care of them. It wasn't always that way, though. Once upon a time, the earth was flat …

In the beginning

When the earth was young, it was flat and everything lived on the flat brown ground together: the sun, the moon, the stars, and the animals. And everything had its own place to stay. Sun lived in a cave, where it went to sleep at night. Moon lived in a black pot, and let his light out when the gods lifted its lid. And all the animals – the elephants, the lions, the buffaloes, the hippos, the buck and the birds – shared one big house and the gods above fed them and gave them water.

Man

One day the god Mulungu decided to make Man to share the earth with the animals. He took three handfuls of the soft earth and made three people from it: two men and a woman. One of the men was a leper. 'I have been sent to save you,' the leper said to the other man and woman. 'But soon I am going to die. Once you have returned me to Mother Earth, go to the river and get some water. Then give thanks by sprinkling my body with it.'

When he died, the couple did as they were told and sprinkled water on his grave. When they returned the next day, they were amazed to find that instead of a grave there were fields of millet, of maize and of grass. 'Hurrah!' they cried. 'The gods have been great. We have hay to make a house. We have maize and millet to eat. Now we can have a family.' So they built a hut from soil and grass, made some porridge from the millet, and soon bore some children. Those children had more children. That is how the earth's first tribe was born.

The sun

One day two men went out exploring the flat earth and came to a cave. Usually caves are dark, but from this one came great rays of heat and light. The men were very frightened. 'What god lives here?' they asked, with terror in their eyes. While one man ran away, the other went in to look. Slowly he crept inside, shielding his eyes from the hot light, until he reached the back, where he saw a huge ball of fire under a stone. It was the sun. 'Man, please help me,' begged the sun, great flames coming from its mouth. 'A stone fell on me, trapping all my power, and I can't escape. I will bring you great luck if you do.' Once the sun had promised he wouldn't burn the man, the man lifted the stone, and out flew the sun, with bright trails of sparks and black smoke and roaring flames behind it. It flew and flew until it reached the great lake in the sky, where it still lives today. It kept its promise to Man, and every day it brings light and warmth to the earth, in thanks for the day Man set him free.

The stars

One day the children were playing on a beach full of stones. 'Watch out,' warned an old man walking by. 'A small stone is as great as a big rock.' Puzzled, the children looked at him and continued their game. Five minutes later, he returned to see a little pebble whizz through the air and hit a girl hard on the head. As she fell to the ground, the pebble flew up into the sky where it exploded into a ball of light. It was the first star ever. 'From now on,' said the old man, 'every time a little child dies, a star will light up in the sky at night.' And until today, it has.

The moon

In the same tribe lived a man called Machelenga who owned a big pot. This was no ordinary pot, for inside it he kept the moon. Every day, as he went to the fields, he warned his children not to touch it. 'The child who touches that pot will have terrible luck,' he said. 'It is a most magical pot. So keep your hands off.'

But one night, when Machelenga was out in the fields, one of the children decided to have a peek inside. 'I've touched it, I've seen it, I've smelt that pot, I can tell you right now that it's not even hot!' he boastfully said to his friends. With that, he marched up to the big black pot and picked up the lid. Moon was delighted! He was sick of the confines of the little black space, and with a whoosh of white light, he swooped out into the black night.

Out in the fields, the father knew at once what had happened. 'You wicked children!' he said, running back to his house. 'Gather ladders for we must catch it. Quick, quick!' After such a long time crammed up in a pot, Moon was not very practised at rising in the sky. By the time the children had found ladders, he had risen only to the top of the first mountain. 'We can catch him, Father, we can catch him!' shouted the children, racing to the mountains. 'Just wait!'

The child who had let Moon out was in the biggest hurry, as he knew how much trouble he was going to be in. He climbed as fast as his little legs could carry him until at last he was at the top, with Moon just above his fingertips. 'I've got him, Father, I've got him,' he cried, and leapt from the top of the ladder towards Moon.

Moon, though, was far too bright to be caught again. Just as the child leapt upwards, it rose even higher into the sky. The child's hands slipped through the air, and he fell slowly onto the steep, rocky mountainside.

The father and mother wept and prayed to Moon to help them to save their child. But it was too late. The child had died. 'Because of your stupid Moon, we have lost our precious child', the wife wailed. 'I am going to live somewhere else where I will never see your Moon again.' And off she went.

She has never stopped travelling, for wherever she goes Moon follows. And Machelenga has never stopped crying. Whenever it is full moon, listen. You are sure to hear him howling.

The rain

When the earth was young, the skies were full of lightning. It would light up the sky day after day, striking down man after man. Every week there was another funeral, until at last the people got angry with God. 'Every week we have to have a funeral,' they shouted, 'and every week we have to provide food and water for the mourners. If you are going to kill us, at least help with the refreshments.'

The god Mulungu apologised for the lightning and promised he would be more helpful in future. 'Now when I send lightning, I will also send rain for you to drink,' he said. 'And I will thunder, too, to bid my own farewells to the dead.' And ever since, he has.

When Hippo was hairy

Told to me in Shona by Cosam Kachembere in Harare, Zimbabwe

In the days when the earth was young, Mvuu, the hippo, was considered to be the most beautiful of all African animals. His large, muscular body was covered with a dark glossy coat. From his head hung a pair of the longest, silkiest ears in the animal kingdom. And from his well-rounded bottom hung the sweetest, shapeliest tail that any animal had ever seen.

Everyone admired Mvuu, from the emerald-coloured sunbirds and naughty monkeys to the mighty King Lion. Across the jungle, as the handsome hippo walked from grassy snack to grassy snack, the creatures would sing out in praise of God's most beautiful creation. 'Mister Mvuu, how beautiful are you!' cried the monkeys from the trees. 'Mighty Mvuu, how handsome are you!' roared the lions. 'Magical Mvuu, we wish we were you!' sang the sunbirds.

Soon Hippo began to believe that he was, indeed, the most beautiful thing on earth. Every morning, when he went for his dawn drink, he would stand by the river, admiring his own reflection and remind himself of his magnificence. 'It's no wonder I'm a jungle obsession,' he would say vainly, tossing his shiny hair in the morning mist. 'It's quite clear that when God wanted perfection, He made me.'

For a while, the other animals put up with Hippo's vanity because he was such a picture to look at. But soon it began to annoy them – especially when he started to make nasty comments about them.

'Bad luck about your bulgy eyes,' he'd say snidely to the chameleon. Or 'Pity about your warty face,' he'd remark rudely to the warthog.

The final straw came one day when Hare was passing by. 'Poor creature,' said Hippo, as he watched Hare hop. 'Such a spindly little frame, and such silly floppy ears. And then, the misfortune of such bent-up back legs. The gods must have been crazy when they created him!'

Now, as we all know, hares have very fine hearing, and this one wasn't at all happy with Hippo's horrible remarks. 'He might be beautiful on the outside, but he is turning rather rotten inside,'

muttered the miffed hare. 'I am going to have to think of a way to sort him out.' And off he hopped to have a think.

Later that day, Hippo was rather surprised to see Hare carrying large bundles of grass towards his house. 'What are you doing?' asked Hippo with a frown. 'Oh, beautiful Mvuu, I am building a fence just for you,' replied Hare. 'Then once you are inside, you won't get dust on your glossy hide.'

Hippo was very pleased. Hare might be ugly, he thought, but he certainly was clever. That night he wandered happily towards his newly fenced house, knowing that in the morning his coat would be even more beautiful, and even glossier.

Once Hippo was settled for the night, Hare crept off to a nearby village. The villagers were sitting round a fire, entranced by a storyteller's tale. And, while their attention was on the story, Hare silently crept beside the fire, stole a burning branch and raced off. When he got to Hippo's new fence, he flung the burning branch onto it and hid behind a nearby tree to watch.

Flames soon flickered skyward, setting fire to everything in their path, including Hippo. 'Help! Help!' cried the mighty Mvuu, as the flames leapt on to his precious coat. 'My ears! My tail! My neck! My face! Help me, oh help me get out of this place!'

Hippo was not a fast runner in those days, but with such scorching flames searing his flesh, the fat creature was soon racing down to the river at the speed of a cross crocodile. When he got there, he jumped in with a mighty splash, and stayed underwater while the cool, wet water soothed his sore, blistered skin.

Mvuu stayed in the water all night, until dawn, when at last he started to feel better. The pain had died down. His tail had stopped throbbing. And even his big bottom had stopped burning. Slowly, he raised his big belly from the river bed, and blowing bubbles, floated up to the surface. Then he got out of the water, and took his normal position on the riverbank, where there was a great pool of water to admire himself in.

But what a shock he got! Rather than the gorgeous, glossy, graceful Mvuu he had been, the creature in the reflection was a stumpy, rather ugly, animal, with no hair at all. Gone was his beautiful, glossy coat. In the place of his long ears were two stubby lumps. At the top of his bottom was a tiny, stubby, fat little tail. His body was covered with a thick, grey skin, with rather nasty patches of pink where the flames had burnt deep.

With a miserable snort, Mvuu threw himself into the river. And there he has remained ever since, coming out only at night when the other animals can't see him. Occasionally, you'll hear him weep when he sees other animals come to admire their own reflections. If you listen carefully, you'll hear him.

'Boooohuhuhuhu,' he'll cry mournfully, 'Boooohuhuhuhu.'

The talking tummy

Told to me in Shona by Cecilia Masekereya in Mabvuku, Zimbabwe

Long ago, there was a drought. There was no fruit on the trees. The green grass turned brown and died. Even the sausage tree stopped making its delicious long green sausage pods. There was nothing on the ground to eat but stones and dust.

The animals were so hungry that King Lion decided to call a meeting. 'Someone has to have an idea what we can do,' he said. So, one day, all of the animals gathered under the shade of the acacia tree. Most of them had never seen a drought, so didn't know what to do. Others, like Elephant, had seen several – when food didn't grow the whole year and rain only fell twice during summer. So it was to them that the animals turned.

'Nzou, Nzou, what should we do?' they sang to the elephants. 'The rain has not come, there are no clouds in the sky, the only thing left is to lie down and die.'

The elephants, being clever creatures, didn't stand for silly sentimentality. 'What nonsense, foolish fellows,' trumpeted the enormous bull elephant. 'We will have to do what Man does. When he can't find food, he grows it.'

The animals erupted in a mass of disdainful bellows and howls. 'Grow it?' growled Leopard, prowling up and down in disbelief. 'Plough fields?' howled Hyena, cackling with laughter. 'Sow seeds?' giggled Gnu, tossing his mangy fringe.

But King Lion gave a roar. 'If any animal has got a better idea, would he step forward?' he said. Slowly the noise subsided and the stamping stopped, as the animals hung their heads in shame. After a few minutes of silence, the king spoke again. 'Well, Elephant,' he smiled. 'I think you'd better tell us how to do it then.'

Elephant, rather pleased with himself, flicked his trunk into the air and strolled self-importantly to the front of the crowd. When the last giggles and chatters stopped, he began. 'I have seen Man,' he droned, giving an elderly snort every now and then, 'and what he does is this. He clears the bush, then he ploughs, then he sows, then he waters, he weeds and he reaps. He plants a variety of plants, so he has some ready in weeks, while others are still ripening. That way, he has food all summer.'

The animals listened and, when he'd finished, let out a loud cheer and quickly arranged themselves into the groups he ordered: rhinos to clear the bush, buffaloes to pull the plough, baboons to plant the tiny seeds, antelopes to pull up the damaging weeds and elephants to sprinkle little pools of muddy water onto the plants to make them grow. After just one meeting, the animal kingdom was going to become one big animal farm.

The animals worked hard, ploughing and hoeing and weeding and reaping and soon the jungle was a mass of lush, green fields filled with delicious crops. There were golden mealies, fat sweet potatoes, crisp green cabbage and bulging orange pumpkins, which the animals ate for breakfast, lunch and supper. Soon everyone fattened out, coats became glossy again, and mothers began to have plump, happy babies.

Life was great in the jungle until the terrible day Hare went to collect some maize and it wasn't there. Every single maize cob had been stolen and the stalks stood bare. The next day, the turnips were taken.

And the following day the sweet potatoes were stolen. The animals were furious – especially Hare, who had stood guard on the night the turnips had vanished. 'What can I do,' he wondered, 'to catch the thief who is pinching our food?'

All night he tossed and he turned in his burrow, trying to think of a plan to catch the thief. Just as dawn broke, he came up with an idea. 'I know!' he said, hopping up and down in his burrow with glee. 'The pumpkin!'

In the middle of the main field, the animals had grown the most magnificent orange pumpkin. It was large and golden and would be ripe within days. 'It would be a perfect trap for a thief,' Hare decided.

After cutting a small trapdoor and hollowing it out, Hare climbed into the pumpkin. 'He will not be able to resist this,' he smiled, as he sat inside and waited.

Sure enough, once the sun had set, and Owl started twittering and whoooooing, Hare heard footsteps outside the pumpkin. 'It's the thief,' he thought, giggling nervously. It was. But before Hare had time to jump out and attack the creature, the whole pumpkin, with him inside, was put in the creature's big mouth and swallowed.

'Hey, hey, help!' shouted Hare, as he and the pumpkin slid down into the creature's belly. 'Stop thief, stop!'

The creature, terrified of the noise it heard, started running away in panic. But everywhere he went, the noise went too. If he jumped across a river, the noise jumped too. If he climbed a tree, the noise climbed as well. Even when he went home to his wife, the noise went home with him.

The creature was terrified. 'What must I do?' he cried to his cowering wife. 'I've got a devil in my belly!' But his wife had no time to answer, for from the depths of its belly came a dark voice: 'Take me to your king oh thief, or you will get no sleep, take me to your king, oh thief, or I will make you weep!' And from inside its stomach came a thudding and bumping noise as Hare took his fists and punched and thumped.

The creature howled in terror and hollered in pain, until at last he could bear it no more. 'I promise, I promise to take you to the king,' he cried, and he ran as fast as he could all the way to Lion.

When they got there, the creature spoke. 'Oh dear King, help me,' he moaned, holding his tummy. 'Inside my stomach is a voice. It hurts me and it devils me. I have to get it out!'

Before the king had a chance to answer, a voice rose from the creature's stomach. 'King, I am no devil. If you order this creature to open its mouth, you will see who I am when I climb out.' Amazed, the king ordered the creature to do as his tummy had told him. And, sure enough, out of the creature's big mouth scrambled not a devil, but a very wet, pumpkin-covered Hare.

When Hare had wiped all the pumpkin from his face, and opened his eyes, he couldn't believe what he saw. 'Baboon!' Hare exclaimed, staring at the creature who had eaten him. 'You rotten thief!' Rather shamefaced, Baboon admitted that it was he who had stolen not only the pumpkin, but the animals' other crops as well.

After praising Hare for his marvellous thief-catching trick, the king turned to Baboon. 'You have proved to be a lazy and wicked creature who has tricked your hard-working friends,' the king scolded. 'For that, the animals can never forgive you. You must take to the hills for ever.'

Sadly, Baboon walked through the valley and climbed high up on to a hill to live. He has lived there ever since. He occasionally ventures into the valley to steal a cob of maize or a juicy sweet potato from someone's field. But there is one thing he will never, ever steal again: pumpkin. I think you know why.

The man who snored and the man who sang

Told to me in Tonga by Beatrice Shawalala outside Lusaka, Zambia

Many years ago, two men set off on a long journey to a faraway valley. All day they travelled, walking over sharp rocks and swimming through streams, climbing over fallen tree trunks and wading through sharp reeds.

It was a hard journey, and by sunset both men were exhausted, hungry and thirsty. It was also getting dark and they had nowhere to sleep. But at last, they spotted a village: a cluster of thatched huts, a well for water and – even better – a fire with a cooking pot steaming on it.

As they walked towards the village, the chief, in leopard skin pants, came out to greet them. 'Welcome!' he said, smiling. 'You must be hungry – come and eat. You must be thirsty – come and drink. And, please, stay the night. However, you must make one promise.'

The men nodded. 'Of course we will make a promise. What is it?' The chief looked at them with a serious face. 'We will happily give you food, water and a bed for the night. But you must promise not to snore. We are very busy people who need our sleep. So anyone who snores is punished.'

The men both nodded their heads in agreement, then sat down round the fire for a meal of maize meal, chicken and beer. It was a fine feast, and after it, the old villagers gathered round the fire to tell stories – tales of wild animals, hunting trips, brave warriors and wise chiefs. Eventually, when the moon was high in the sky, the men went to their hut and settled down to sleep.

In the middle of the night, one of the men woke up with a terrible fright. There was something in the hut – something that was making a loud roaring, whistling, blowing sound. A terrifying sound! He lay there with his heart beating in his chest and raised his head slowly to look around. There was nothing in the hut but his friend. Yet still the noise rose in the air. 'Nnnnnnnkkkkkkkkhhhho!' it went loudly in the darkness, 'Nnnnnnkkkkkkkkkho!' As the man looked round the hut, he realised what the noise was. 'Oh no!' he exclaimed in the dark. 'My friend is snoring! The chief warned us that anyone who snored would be punished. I must get up and stop him.'

Quickly he rose from his bed to wake his friend, but it was too late. Outside the door he could hear the villagers whispering about the terrible snoring and the punishment the chief was going to inflict.

Before anyone had had a chance to come inside the hut, the man had made a plan. He started to sing.

Slowly, the villagers' whispering stopped and another sound started – the villagers singing along. They sang and they sang. They fetched

their drums, then their whistles. And before long the man could hardly hear his own voice for the party outside. All night the villagers sang and whistled and danced. At last, when dawn came, they all went to bed, tired but happy.

That morning, the snoring man woke up refreshed after a good night's sleep. His friend, however, was exhausted. 'You have no idea how lucky you are that I saved you!' said the tired friend. 'We can't stay here a single night longer, though, for this time the villagers will surely punish us.'

After breakfast, the men packed their bags and went to thank the chief for his hospitality. 'No, no, no,' said the chief, smiling. 'It is we who must thank you. For never before have we heard such sweet songs, or held such a marvellous party. Please, as a thank you, take this gift of gold.' The chief then handed the singing man a leather bag filled with shiny, precious gold.

The two men couldn't believe their luck, and once they had thanked the chief again, they set off on their journey. But as soon as they were out of the village, the snoring man asked his friend to stop. 'I would like my share of the gold now,' he said. 'Let's stop under this shady tree and divide it.'

The singing man was not only tired from having been awake all night, but he was very grumpy. 'What do you mean divide it?' he said crossly to the snoring man. 'If I hadn't sung all night, and whistled and danced and entertained those villagers, they would have had us for supper. All you did is make horrible snoring sounds. It was you who got us into trouble in the first place.'

The snoring man shook his head vigorously and started to shout and wave his fist about. He'd had a good night's sleep and was now full of energy. 'Listen here,' he said, waving his finger at his tired friend's face. 'If it weren't for my snoring, you wouldn't have had to sing in the first place. You would have slept all night. It's thanks to me that you were given the chance to entertain the villagers. Half that gold is mine. Now hand it over!'

No matter how hard the snoring man tugged, the singing man wouldn't hand over the bag. Soon the former friends were wrestling in the mud, pounding and punching and hitting each other.

What they didn't realise is that they were being watched from above. The rain god happened to be passing on his rain clouds in the sky, and he couldn't believe how silly the two men were being. After thundering loudly at the men from above, he shot down a huge bolt of lighting. With a crack! and a bang! it sent the pair whizzing into the air. And with a fizzz! it hit the bag of gold, shooting it like a star into the sky.

Neither of the men ever saw the gold again. The rain god took every little bit and used it to make his rainbow sparkle. But that doesn't stop men from trying to find it. Every time it rains, you will see them heading across the Mrican valley towards the rainbow. Ask them where they are going and they will tell you – to find the singing man's lost bag of gold.

How Honeybird punished the greedy man

Told to me in Ndebele by Isaac Nyatha in Bulawayo, Zimbabwe

The honeybird has always been the friendliest of birds, fetching men from their fields and leading them into the forest to show them where to find honey. 'Chee Chee!' it has called for centuries, 'Follow me! Follow me!' flying in circles around the spot where man could find sweet, golden honeycomb.

One day, long ago, Honeybird found a very large honeycomb that his friends the bees had been working on in the hollow trunk of a tree. He loved honey, but being a kind, sharing creature, he flew straight to the fields to find someone to share his good fortune. At the edge of the forest, in a little clearing, he saw a man busily planting maize seeds in the earth. 'Chee! Chee!' sang Honeybird, flying backwards and forwards over the man's head. 'Chee! Chee! Follow me! Follow me!'

The man had heard of the great honeybird, which led lucky men to a kingdom filled with sweet golden treasure, but he had never seen one with his own eyes. So, quickly, he lay down his spade and seed and followed the bird into the forest.

The man climbed down ditches, over tree trunks and through rivers until at last the bird stopped before a hollow tree where a swarm of bees lived. There, it flew round and round, darting up and down, directing the man exactly where to look.

Staring into the tree, the man couldn't believe his luck. For there, in the dark hollow, was the biggest stash of honey he had ever seen – great layers of golden, dripping combs that overflowed from the trunk and permeating the air with a sweet, flowery smell.

The man was ecstatic, and being rather a greedy chap, he quickly fell to his knees, stretched his hand inside the hole and took out a great big piece of comb, which he stuffed into his mouth. With honey dripping down his chin and running down his arms, he took another, then another, chomping and chewing and slurping and swallowing, until soon there was not a single drop of honey left. After a very noisy burp, he got up, wiped his sticky hands on his trousers and set off, without even bothering to thank the bees, or his guide the honeybird.

Honeybird was furious. 'Chee Chee!' he squawked unhappily after the greedy, rude man. 'Chee Chee! What about me? What about me?' But the man didn't even look up as he rubbed his rounded belly and headed home.

The next morning Honeybird was still so cross about the man's ingratitude that he had an idea that might teach the man a lesson. Flying through the forest, he looked here and looked there until he found exactly what he wanted. There, under a fallen tree in the middle of the forest lay a leopard with her three cubs. Not only was their home shady and protected, but nearby was a supply of dark, rich honey. And, as you probably know, leopards like nothing more than a daily lick of honey.

Once he'd hatched his plan, Honeybird knew exactly what to do: to fly back to the man's field and lure him once again. The man of course was over the moon, for although he was feeling a little sick from too much honey the day before, he couldn't resist the cry. Quickly, he threw down his tools and hurried after the bird.

The journey to the honey was longer this time – over a river, around a hill, through a thick forest and down a narrow path – but at last Honeybird stopped flying, and began to circle a thickly grassed area.

Knowing that meant honey, the man greedily shot forward, his legs stumbling in the grass to get to the fallen tree.

This time, though, there was more than just golden honey waiting for him. Leopard had spotted the fat-tummied human stumbling through the bush from far away, and as the man clumsily stepped on one of her cubs, Leopard leapt forward with a terrifying roar.

With one swipe of her paw, she swatted the man to the ground and bit him hard on the arm. It was not a nice lesson to learn, but Man knows now. Today, whenever he is invited into the animal kingdom, he enters with caution, knowing that the treasures of the forest are for all – creatures great and small.

The race between
Hare and Tortoise

Told to me in Bemba by John Zulu in the Luangwa Valley, Zambia

One morning Tortoise was ambling happily towards the river when he came upon Hare. He wasn't particularly pleased, for he had always thought Hare was rude. But today he was even less pleased than usual by the long-eared creature's snide greeting. 'Morning slowcoach,' sneered Hare, nibbling casually on a piece of grass. 'Can I give you a lift to the river? I would hate you to miss sunset …'

Tortoise narrowed his eyes crossly. 'Actually, Hare,' he said, in a stiff, unamused tone, 'it is I who should be offering you a lift. As every intelligent animal knows, tortoises are fine athletes, particularly over long distances. Even a supposed slowcoach like me could outrun a mere bunny like you.'

Hare laughed. Run? He had never seen Tortoise even jog! But as the creature was so cheeky, there was only one way to find out. 'Well, old man,' he said, 'what about a race?'

Tortoise grinned. Hare had fallen into his trap, and he had planned exactly how he was going to win the race. 'Give me a few days to train,' he said, 'and I will be ready. Shall we say Saturday?' With the date set, Hare hopped off happily.

When Hare was out of sight, Tortoise called his relatives together and told them about the Saturday's race. 'If you want to teach that conceited creature a lesson, you will all have to play a part,' he said.

'Listen carefully, for this is what I want you to do ...' Carefully he explained how each tortoise should hide in bushes along the route of the race, and come out when he was needed. 'We all look the same,' he grinned. 'Hare will never know that you are not me!'

On the day of the race, Hare and Tortoise met under a shady marula tree, watched by a crowd of excited animals. As the pair lined up at the starting post, Fish Eagle gave a screech. 'Go!' he whistled through his sharp yellow beak. 'Run!'

The two creatures ran as fast as their legs would carry them, Hare leaping off, with Tortoise trundling along behind him. After a while Hare became thirsty. 'Given I can't see Slowcoach for dust, I might as well sit for a sip and a snooze,' he said, with a self-satisfied smirk. Stopping, he settled down beneath a shady tree with a calabash of water and soon went to sleep.

After a few minutes, he was awoken by a yell. 'Hey, Long-ears. Bit tired?' he heard. As he opened his eyes, there was Tortoise, jogging freshly along in front of him.

Hare couldn't believe his eyes. How on earth had old short-legs managed to catch up, he wondered. Jumping up with his calabash, he leapt off again, overtaking Tortoise and hopping and jumping as fast as his legs would take him.

He hopped and hopped and hopped, but with the sun beating down on his back, and dust flying into his face, he soon needed to stop. In the shade of a tree, he uncorked his calabash and lifted it to his mouth. But no sooner had he had a single gulp than a yell passed by. 'See you at the finish, Hare!' shouted a voice. Hare couldn't believe his ears, so he lowered his calabash and looked with his eyes. His ears weren't tricking him. The brown flash was indeed Tortoise!

Panicking, Hare leapt up and was soon hopping and leaping over logs and through grass. At last he saw the long, green river – where the finish line had been set. 'Thank goodness for that!' he sighed, as little beads of sweat slipped from his fur. 'The end!'

He slowed down, and closing his eyes imagined the medal being put round his neck and the animal kingdom gathering round to offer their congratulations. 'How wonderful it will be,' he smiled, 'to be the fastest jumper in the jungle!' But as he looked forward his heart sank. For just before the finish line, about to cross it, was Tortoise.

A roar went up from the watching crowd of animals and the skies were filled with happy cries and shrieks and howls and yowls as Tortoise slowly crossed the line. 'Well done, Shelled One!' yelled Giraffe, waving his neck about excitedly. 'King of the Road!' trumpeted Elephant, stamping his feet till dust rose in the sky.

As Tortoise was patted on his shell and a medal hung about his scaly neck, Hare had to admit he had been well and truly beaten. 'You have talents, Tortoise, that I had never imagined,' he said shamefacedly, his ears flopping down with embarrassment. 'From this day forward, I will never tease you again.'

The Tortoise looked at him, smiling wisely. 'My relatives and I are delighted to hear it, Hare,' he said. And off he went for a great celebration – of the greatest tortoise relay team that ever lived.

The princess and the python

Told to me in Shona by Mason Kanjanda in Harare, Zimbabwe

One day, long ago, birds flying over the palace of Zimbabwe heard a beautiful girl's voice rising in the sky. Her song was sweet, but it was also sad. 'Help me oh Moon God to be brave; for I have to go to the python's cave,' the song went.

The birds looked over the stone wall of the king's palace and there they saw their friend, the Buhera Princess, weeping in the sun. 'What is wrong,' the birds asked. 'My father is very ill, and we have tried everything to make him well,' she replied. 'The most famous witch doctors have come from all over the kingdom, we have sacrificed cows to the Moon God and our ancestors' spirits, and we have piled our altars with maize and melons. But nothing has worked. Now, my brothers say, I have to go to visit the great python in the cave to beg him to heal my father, the king. They have already been to the snake and returned with nothing but fear. I am the last hope.'

The birds twittered with horror. The python's cave! Every creature knew what happened in that dark black hole. Things went in, but never came out. How was a young, beautiful princess going to succeed when so many other strong men had failed?

'No, no, no, you can't go!' they shrieked. But the Princess was insistent. 'My heart has so much love for my father that it has no space for fear,' she said. 'I must.' And down the path she walked, singing with the birds to give her courage.

After a long walk in the sun the princess reached the creature's cave. Nervously she peered inside until she saw a great black head with yellow eyes shining out. 'Who interrupts my s-s-s-s-sleep?' hissed the python, its fangs glistening in the sunlight. 'Do you not know, Princess-s-s-s-s, that my favourite food is people? Can you not see footprints-s-s-s in the s-s-s-sand of brave warriors who have fled?'

The princess looked at the scaly creature with tears in her eyes. 'Please, mighty Python,' she cried. 'My father, the king, is dying. Only you, the great healer, can make him well. I beg of you, on behalf of our kingdom, save him.'

The python looked at her through his narrow yellow eyes. 'S-s-s-s-sing to me,' he hissed, 'and carry me coiled round your body to your father. Your s-s-s-sweet voice will be my payment.'

The birds, sitting in the trees, started to screech and cry. 'Don't listen, Princess, don't listen!' they shrieked. 'That's how he kills people, by coiling round them and squeezing them to death. Run!'

But the princess stood tall as she had been taught by her father, her eland cloak round her shoulders and her gold and ostrich necklace glinting in the sun. 'Come, Magic One,' she said, 'Come.' Slowly the great snake started to slither out of his cave and wind his long, slippery body round hers, until the princess was completely entwined by cold python skin.

When they saw the python coming, the villagers ran away in fear, until they heard the princess's sweet voice. 'Loosen your arrows, and drop your bows,' she commanded, as the warriors came towards her. 'I bring a great serpent to heal the sick king.'

But the princess stood tall as she had been taught by her father, her eland cloak round her shoulders and her gold and ostrich necklace glinting in the sun. 'Come, Magic One,' she said, 'Come.' Slowly the great snake started to slither out of his cave and wind his long, slippery body round hers, until the princess was completely entwined by cold python skin.

When they saw the python coming, the villagers ran away in fear, until they heard the princess's sweet voice. 'Loosen your arrows, and drop your bows,' she commanded, as the warriors came towards her. 'I bring a great serpent to heal the sick king.'

The warriors did as she said and the python uncoiled itself from her body and slithered into her father's house. Soon the palace was filled with smoke and smells and herbs, as the princess made a fire and brought out Python's amulets of healing oils and herbs so that he could make his potion. When a powerful smoke filled the air, the serpent took the mixture off the fire and spoon by spoon fed it the king. Mter twelve spoonfuls, the king sat up. Then slowly he got out of bed and walked. He was healed.

The village erupted as the villagers sang, whistled and shrieked praises to the python. The king fell to his knees before the great serpent. 'You have saved me,' he said, 'and in thanks I would like you to live among us as our Royal Village Healer. Will you stay?'

Python shook his head. 'I am a creature of the jungle and my place is my cave,' he hissed. 'The princess must now take me back.' Quietness once again descended on the village as the snake wound itself again about her tiny body. Then, with his head resting on her shoulder, they set off into the jungle, her voice rising into the air as she sang songs of praise to the python.

At the cave, the serpent unwound itself. Then, turning to the princess, it invited her in. 'No, no, no!' screeched the birds overhead. 'He will squeeze you, he will squish you, he will bite you and eat you!' But the princess ignored them. 'You have saved my father, so I am sure youwill not harm me, dear friend. Thank you,' she said, and followed him into the darkness.

The cave was nothing like she had expected. Rather than a dark hole littered with warriors' skulls and bones, with bats flying about, the cave glistened with treasure. Great clay pots spilled jewels out on to rocks. Gold beads lay on the floor. Eland skins hung on the walls. And on a ledge lay a finely beaded wrap of silk.

Python looked at her fondly. 'You have shown the kindness and strength of a great woman,' he hissed. 'Please, take what you like. What is mine is yours.' Hanging her head shyly, the girl replied as the queen had taught her. 'Thank you Python,' she said politely, 'but I can only accept a single gift. And that must be chosen by you.'

Looking round, the python picked the finest necklace the princess had ever seen – a string of moonstones and opals which reflected the light of her god, the moon. Hanging them gently from his fangs, he slithered over to her and put them in her outstretched hands. After putting them round her neck and thanking him, she bid him farewell, and joined her friends the birds outside for the journey home.

But that wasn't the end of the princess's happy tale. When she got back to the kingdom, her father was so pleased that his brave daughter was safe, he made her ruler of his kingdom. 'Your necklace is proof to man and woman of your courage and wisdom,' he said. 'You, my princess, are now Queen.'

To crown her joy, at the celebrations the next day, a handsome stranger came by with caskets of gifts for her – of gold, gems, skins and silk. Then he asked for her hand in marriage. 'I am a prince,' he said, 'who has been trapped in a python's skin. Only the love and kindness of a great woman could save me – and that is you, dear Princess. Will you marry me so our great tribes can be joined as one?'

The princess happily agreed and the pair sat on their carved wooden thrones while their kingdom celebrated with feasts, and singing and dancing. The tribe still lives today, near the remnants of their ancient palace. Should you meet their queen, ask to see her necklace. It is made of moonstone – the gift given to her ancestor long ago by the python prince.

This moonstone necklace, which symbolised luck and fertility to the moon-worshipping Buhera clan, actually existed and was worn by the chieftainess of the clan, who handed it down to the next chief's eldest daughter.

The man with big lips

Told to me in Shona by Amon Sithole
in Harare, Zimbabwe

Once upon a time by the side of a river lived a man with very big lips. Every day, as the women of his village passed him fishing on the riverbank, they would giggle and call out. 'Jindwe Long Lips! Who would ever marry you? No one would want to watch those fat lips chew!'

Jindwe naturally was upset. It was true – he did have enormous lips, he muttered to himself, but it was hardly his fault. 'As my mother always said "Your heart is big, your brain is sharp, your body is strong and you are the kindest man in the village. So don't take any notice." But girls do take notice,' he sighed, sadly casting his fishing line into the water.

One day Jindwe was fishing as usual when his rod suddenly bent. 'This must the king of all fish!' he thought excitedly. For almost an hour he fought the fish, as it fought and thrashed in the water. Then, just as he was about to reel it in, it tangled itself in some reeds. As much as Jindwe tugged and tussled, he couldn't free the fish. It was stuck.

Jindwe didn't like losing a fish, and he could not afford to lose his precious hook and line. So, lying down his rod on the riverbank, he took hold of the line and followed it into the water. Imagine his horror when in front of him in the water, staring frostily, was Crocodile, King of the River.

Jindwe started to walk backwards. 'Pardon me entering your kingdom, King Crocodile,' said Jindwe shaking, his eyes wide with terror. 'But I am searching for a large fish who has swum away with my hook. Did you see it go by?'

Crocodile was usually a mean green fish-eating machine. But today, he was in a good mood and flattered by this man's manners. 'Since you have been so polite, young man,' said Crocodile, staring with his yellow eyes, 'I will give you magical powers to find it. Keep walking underwater and I will ensure you can breathe. Enjoy your journey.' Then he disappeared.

Jindwe didn't know whether King Crocodile was tricking him or not. But, desperate to find his hook, he slowly walked into the deep water to look. And just as the king had promised, he could breathe.

It was wonderful being able to stroll along the riverbed, past colourful little river crabs, to wave to the fat-whiskered barbel and to watch the silky green reeds flutter against his skin, and Jindwe was very happy. As he walked contentedly round a bend in the river, he came upon a hut with a dirty old lady sitting outside, her skin caked with mud and her weedy green hair hanging around her face. 'Good day, old lady,' he said politely, as his mother had taught him. 'Have you seen a fish pass by with a hook and line?'

The old lady looked puzzled. 'Are you wandering about looking for a single hook?' she cackled. 'Then you must be a very poor man indeed. This is dangerous territory where no man has ventured before. Do you not know there are crocodiles here?'

Jindwe nodded. 'I do know of the dangers, old woman,' he said. 'But I am a poor man who cannot even afford a wife. So a little hook means a lot to me. Besides,' he sighed, 'no one will marry me anyway because of my big lips.'

The old woman took pity on him. He had such a kind face. And a lovely smile. She wanted to help him, but before she did so, she decided to test him. 'I'm an old, old woman and cannot reach my

back to wash it,' she said. 'It is now so dirty that even fish are starting to nibble on it. Would you mind giving it a clean?'

Jindwe, being a kind man, agreed and, taking a spongy plant from the river bed, he set about cleaning the thick layers of green slime, knobbly weeds and slithery water snails off her back. When he'd finished, her back was so smooth that even the fish came to look at themselves in its shiny surface. 'Thank you, Jindwe,' smiled the woman, her facing cracking into a thousand wrinkles. 'You are indeed a fine man, and will be rewarded richly.'

She then disappeared into her hut and brought out six small pumpkins which she handed to him. Jindwe was very pleased. Even if he didn't find his fish, he thought, at least he would have something for supper. He thanked the woman, put the pumpkins in his pouch and prepared to go home. But before he went, the old woman gave him a warning. 'Be aware, young man, that these are not normal pumpkins,' she said. 'Fill them with water as soon as they break, and you will be richly rewarded. But let them dry out and they will die with you.'

Jindwe nodded and after he had said goodbye, he started his ascent out of the water and on to the path home. As he walked along, he heard a great crash behind him. 'Oh no!' he thought, turning round, 'A pumpkin has fallen out!' He turned round to pick it up, but instead of a pumpkin on the ground, there stood a beautiful girl on the pumpkin shell.

Jindwe had never seen such a beautiful girl, and as he stared, spellbound at her long dark hair and soft skin, she started falling to the floor. 'Water! Water!' she sighed, lying on the ground. 'Please, my dear husband, get me water!' Quickly, Jindwe ran back to the river. But he was too late. By the time he got back to the girl, all that was left on the path was a pumpkin shell with a shrivelled pumpkin flower lying nearby.

Jindwe was terribly upset. The girl had been beautiful. And she had called him husband – something no one had ever called him before.

'I now know what the old lady meant,' he thought. 'Make sure you fill them with water as soon as they break, and you will be richly rewarded for ever.'

Picking up his bag of five pumpkins, Jindwe ran back to the river. One by one, he took them out and cracked them open on a rock, filling each with water as they split. As he did so, five maidens appeared, each more beautiful than he'd ever seen. 'We are the daughters of the crocodile king,' they said, 'and we have been sent by his wife, the Old Lady of the River, as thanks for your kindness and by our father for your politeness. If you accept us as your wives, we will love and care for you forever.'

Jindwe was overjoyed, and together the six of them walked back to his small hut. Inside, each maiden took a turn in showing her new husband her magical skills. 'I can spin wild cotton,' said the first, showing him a piece of soft cloth. 'I weave palm baskets,' said the second, presenting him with a finely patterned beer basket. 'I am magic and will bring rain to your crops,' said the third. 'I will tend your crops, keep your house and cook dishes for your delight,' said the fourth, smiling and showing him her muscles.

Finally, the last princess looked at him shyly. 'I am the Star of Fertility,' she smiled. 'I will make your flocks expand and your crops blossom, and every autumn I will bear a son or daughter to bring pride to your kingdom.'

Jindwe's big lips stretched into a happy smile. 'We are blessed,' he said, 'and between us we will make our people mighty.'

He was right. Today, there are many of Jindwe's ancestors throughout Africa. He became a great king, and his story of his crocodile daughters is known throughout the lands. Now everyone wants big lips. It is a sign that you are a descendant of one of the earth's greatest kings – Jindwe, the keeper of Big Lips and a Big Heart, and the only man who has ever been rewarded by a crocodile.

The long-eared thief

Told to me in Shona by Pastor John Chirenje in Kwekwe, Zimbabwe

Once upon a time a famine overcame the land. Rain didn't fall, the skies were clear and the sun shone so brightly it baked the earth red and dry. There were only muddy puddles to drink, and dry sticks to eat. It was a terrible time for the animals.

One day King Elephant (as he was then) called his kingdom to a meeting to decide what to do. 'My dear creatures,' he said ponderously, his trunk waving this way and that. 'We have to face it. Not one of us is a farmer, really, but at times like this we don't have a choice. Either we starve to death or we try to grow something. What do you say?'

'Farm?' roared the animals, as a great guffaw filled the air, monkeys tittering, antelopes hooting, hyenas giggling and lions roaring. 'We're wild animals, Elephant – we don't farm!'

Elephant wasn't pleased. 'Silence,' he trumpeted, stamping his great front foot, sending dust flying. 'If anyone has a better idea, come forward.' But no one did have a better idea. Everyone had already tried their ideas – and failed. 'Right then. See you first thing tomorrow by the river,' snorted Elephant, rather pleased with himself.

The summer passed and, thanks to their marvellous vegetable patch of fat pumpkins, golden maize and sweet potatoes, the animals fattened up. All of them but one, that is. Hare, being a bit of an arrogant, lazy creature, had decided farming was below a clever, fast, crafty creature like him. So, while the animals were toiling in their soil, lazy Hare lay about.

At first Hare had more than enough food – he chomped happily on roots beneath the ground and nibbled on acorns or bits of bark. But when his ribs began to show, he knew he had to make a plan.

One day, when he was on the path back to his burrow, Hare bumped into Honeybadger carrying a great pot of honey. 'Dear friend Honeybadger, cleverest animal in the kingdom,' whispered Hare in a snivelly, mousy voice. 'I have had so little food that I am almost fainting with hunger. Could you possibly help me?' Honeybadger, looking at Hare's bony ribs, grudgingly parted with his pot of the yummiest, scrummiest honey Hare had ever seen. But he didn't intend to eat it. 'The animals will never be able to resist this as a bribe,' he smiled, licking his sticky lips as he hopped along.

That night Hare crept to the fields with his pot of honey and, as he had predicted, beside the animals' crops Impala stood guard. 'Who goes there?' harruphed Impala. 'It is only I, the Hare, with my pot of golden honey,' said Hare sweetly. Impala pricked up his ears. 'Honey?' he snorted, a touch of envy in his voice. 'Yes, I've been given it to guard,' said Hare. 'My friends are allowed to sip it on one condition: that their legs and arms are tied up first. It is so sweet, you see, that whoever tastes it might wrench it from me to get more.'

Impala, naturally, could not resist tasting such a superior honey. So soon Hare was tying the silly creature's legs together, before lowering the honey pot to Impala's mouth. 'This honey is heavenly!' Impala sighed, closing his eyes and slowly licking little dribbles of golden liquid dripping from his chin. 'May I have one more sip, Hare?' But when he looked up, Hare was no longer there. The cunning creature had hopped off into the maize patch, and he was comfortably chomping the animal kingdom's great golden cobs.

'Stop thief!' shouted Impala, snorting and screeching and wriggling and waggling his tied-up legs in the dust. But there was nothing he could do. Hare had well and truly trussed him up. So there he lay, until the next day.

When dawn came and the animals arrived at the field, they were furious to see their maize plants bare. 'Greedy Impala,' trumpeted Elephant. 'Useless antelope,' howled Wild Dog. 'Stupid creature!' screeched Monkey.

As the shame-faced impala was untied, honey still dripping from its lips, Elephant picked another animal to stand on guard: Hyena. 'At least hyenas eat meat and won't be tempted by Hare's honey tricks,' said Elephant crossly, picking up a few stray cobs of maize Hare had left lying on the ground as he stomped off.

All night Hyena stood guarding the crops. It was tiring and tedious work and Hyena could feel his eyelids slowly drooping downwards. Just as he was dozing off, under his nose wafted the sweetest smell he'd ever encountered: a mix of roses and oranges and roasted nuts and marula fruits. Mmmmmn! he purred. When he opened his eyes, under his nose was a huge pot of honey. And Hare.

'Why hello my dear friend Hyena,' said Hare smilingly. 'How splendid to see you under such a fabulous full moon. Can I tempt you to a sweet sip?' Hyena knew he should say no to Hare's smooth tricks, but the nearer his nose got to the luscious liquid, the less he could resist. 'Go on, then, tie me up for one sip,' he ordered Hare. 'But make it quick.'

So, just as Hyena had requested, Hare took the rope from his pocket, tied Hyena's four legs up, and gave him a sip of honey. While Hyena's eyes were rolling in delight at the delicious honey, the long-eared scoundrel scampered off into the maize.

What Hare had forgotten is that Hyena can make the most horrific noise when he wants to – wild whooooooooops and witchlike cackles that would wake any slumbering creature. And cross hyenas make the worst sounds of all. When this one realised he had been tricked, he set his vocal cords free, hollering and howling and cackling and whooping for all his might, waking every creature from their jungle beds and sending them running into the fields.

Hare, hearing the crashing and crackling of breaking branches as animals tore through the bush, knew his stealing days were over. As fast as his legs would take him, he hopped away – under logs, through grass, over springs and along muddy paths – until he came to the muddy puddles of the river. Animals didn't normally go near this part, for there lived a tribe of ever-hungry crocodiles. But crafty Hare once more had a plan.

'Quick crocodiles, line up,' panted the sly scoundrel. 'The king is coming to count all the creatures of his kingdom and he has ordered me to order you to get in a line.' The crocodiles, hearing the great crashing of branches approaching the river, believed that King Elephant was indeed coming. So, nose to tail, they lined up from one side of the riverbank to the other.

No sooner had they done it than Hare sprung from the riverbank onto their backs and was hopping, crocodile to crocodile, until he reached the other side. 'Thanks crocodiles, for making a bridge,' he said, giving a happy little whoop as he landed on the other bank. 'Tricked you as well!'

The crocodiles snapped and lashed their tails in anger when they realised their sleep had been disturbed by a long-eared lying Hare, but it was too late. He had escaped. And when the rest of the animals arrived, puffing and panting, and scratched by branches and thorns, Hare had vanished. And the crocodile crossing had vanished too.

No matter how loudly they harrumphed and snorted and trumpeted with frustration, there was nothing the animals could do. Once more Hare had tricked them. Yet again, he had stolen from them. And as ever, he had got away with it. Why? Because he's clever. And all the animals in the jungle know: Clever wins!

The lion, the snake and
the man

Told to me in Shona by
Maureen Chirembwe in Mabvuku, Zimbabwe

Once upon a time a man called Mufakise was walking through the forest on the way to his field when he heard a strange noise. Hisssssssss! It whistled into the sky. Roarrrrrrr! It rose into the clouds. Heeeeeeey! It shouted towards the sun. Cupping his ear, Mufakise walked towards the sound until he reached a deep, dark pit.

'Who are you that hisses, roars and shouts?' Mufakise stammered nervously, as he peered into the darkness. 'Tell me your name and what you're shouting about.'

From the pit came a thin, weedy voice, obviously tired of shouting. 'Thank goodness you have come, kind man,' it said. 'We have fallen into a pit and can't get out.'

Mufakise crept forward and leant over the edge. Sure enough, in the darkness beneath the surface of the earth, stood a man, a lion and a snake.

Mufakise wasn't quite sure what to do – or who to help first. 'If I help the lion he might eat me before I rescue the others,' he reasoned. 'If I help the snake he might bite me. The sensible thing, I suppose, would be to help the man. The man like me.'

Kneeling at the edge of the pit, he lowered his arm into the darkness and offered the man a hand up. Gripping it tightly, the man pulled on it, scrambled up, and then vanished into the forest. 'Not even a word of thanks,' muttered Mufakise. 'And he was a man. A man like me.'

Shaking his head at the man's bad manners, Mufakise put his hand down to help the snake. Unlike the man, the snake was delighted by Mufakise's help. 'Thankkkkkkkksssss, Mufakissssse, you are a man amongst men,' it hissed happily, slithering around his feet with joy. 'One day I shall return the favour. I will not forget.'

Finally, pleased with the snake's manners, Mufakise pulled the lion out. He, too, was delighted with the man's help. 'Mufakise, you are a marvel,' he purred happily. 'You will not regret this. And one day I shall return the favour.' And off he trotted.

Mufakise, feeling pleased at his three good deeds, spent the rest of his day happily tending his fields. At sunset, he put down his tools and walked home to make his supper. But instead of his usual empty hut, there, sitting in the sun, was Lion, accompanied by a beautiful girl and a herd of fat brown cows.

Lion greeted him with a friendly roar before explaining his visit. 'A lion always keeps its promise and I said I would return your favour,' he rumbled. 'Please accept the chief's daughter as your wife, and the finest herd in the land as a gift from me.'

Mufakise couldn't believe his luck and thanked the Lion. 'You have rewarded me richly,' he said. 'I will never forget that. Or the rudeness of the man, the man like me.'

The next day, when Mufakise returned home to his new wife and his cows, another guest was waiting. This time it was Snake, with a little leather bag of magic herbs to cure snakebite. 'A snake always keeps its word, and I said I would return the favour,' he hissed. 'Always carry this magic bag and you will have the power to save anybody.'

Again, Mufakise thanked his animal friend and put the bag of herbs on a leather thong round his neck. 'What manners Snake has to reward me so richly,' he marvelled again. 'They are so much better than Man's, the man like me.'

Unbeknown to Mufakise, the man actually lived in the next village to him. One day a royal messenger arrived there with a notice from the king. 'My daughter has vanished, and my royal herd,' the royal proclamation said. 'The man who returns them will be richly rewarded.'

The man was very excited, for he had heard that Mufakise had a beautiful new wife and a herd of fine cows. 'They must be the king's,' he thought excitedly and ran to the palace to report his suspicions. That night the king's soldiers arrived at Mufakise's hut. And sure enough, the man was right. Mufakise was living with the chief's daughter, and in his kraal were the king's royal herd. At once the soldiers arrested Mufakise and marched him off to jail.

As he lay on the hard jail floor that night, cold and miserable, Mufakise heard a hiss. There, in a corner, was Snake. 'Mufakise, you have been wronged,' he hissed. 'You have been wronged by the man, the man like you. So we animals have made a plot to put it right.' Then he vanished into the night.

The puzzled Mufakise went to sleep and was woken the next day by shouting outside the jail. 'The king has been bitten by a snake and is dying,' the voice said. 'Whoever can save him will be richly rewarded.'

Mufakise felt around his neck. There, on a leather thong, hung the magic pouch of herbs Snake had given him. 'Thank you, Snake,' he smiled. 'For I can now save the king.'

Mufakise called the guards, and after he had showed them his magic herbs, they marched him off to the king's kraal. The king lay almost dead on his bed, but just as the snake had promised, once Mufakise had applied the herbs to the snakebite, the king's eyes opened. Soon his fever broke and he could sit up. He was saved.

'Oh great healer of men,' the king said, holding Mufakise's hand. 'You have saved my life. And for that you will be richly rewarded. What would you like?'

Mufakise looked at him happily. 'Oh great King, I have three favours to ask: that I am reunited with your daughter, who is my beloved wife, that you let me look after your fat brown cows again, and that your tribe stops hunting Lion and Snake. They are the kings of creatures, and it is thanks to them that we are all happy and well.'

The king agreed and Mufakise was soon reunited with his wife and their cows and sent home with great riches. From that day on, the man, the lion and the snake have lived happily ever after.

The lion men

Told to me in Shona by poet Chirikure Chirikure, in Harare, Zimbabwe, and Janet Pakwenda, a subsistence farmer from Fringilla, outside Lusaka, Zambia. Also told in Bemba by Delina Ngulube, a leper, at the Latete leper colony in Zambia

Many years ago in the golden valleys of Africa lived a man and wife, their three beautiful daughters and a young son. The daughters were known throughout their valley for their pretty brown eyes, slender ankles, soft skin and kind hearts. Every month, local suitors would flock to the girls' father to ask for their hand in marriage. But every time they would be turned away, disappointed. The girls simply refused to get married if it meant being parted from one another. 'If we get married, we will marry together,' they vowed.

One evening, as the girls sat round the fire, three handsome young men appeared from the forest wearing lion skins around their waists. They were the tallest, strongest warriors the girls had ever seen and quickly the girls pulled up their best wooden stools and invited the men to sit and eat with them.

The men explained that they were from a magical kingdom far away, where the hills were as blue as the sky, and the water as sweet as honey. Food, they said, was plentiful. The children were healthy and fat. And the women were so content that every day the air was filled with happy song. 'The only thing missing in our lives,' they said, 'is beautiful brides like you. And that is why we are here. We have come to ask whether you would do us the honour of marrying us?'

The girls were very excited. At last they could get married and all stay together. They could be sisters as well as sisters-in-law! Their children would grow up together. It was perfect. But there was a problem. Their parents had always warned them of strangers – especially those from unknown kingdoms. They would definitely not agree to these foreign young men taking their precious daughters. There was only one solution: to run away. Quietly, by the light of the moon, the three girls packed a small bundle of belongings, and crept away by the light of the moon with their new husbands.

What the girls hadn't counted on was their little brother spying on them from behind a rock. Like most little brothers, he didn't want to be left out of anything, and soon he was stamping his feet and shouting. 'I'm your protector, so take me too,' he screeched. 'If you don't I'll fetch father to come and get you!'

The girls didn't like the idea of taking their little brother, but they certainly didn't want him to wake their father. So, making him promise to keep quiet, they agreed, and quickly set off on their journey. For three days and three nights the seven of them walked through kraals and over koppies, climbed rocks and waded rivers. On the fourth day they came to the most beautiful valley they had ever seen.

While the girls were overawed with the blue mountains, the clear streams, and the orchards of wild fruit trees, they were even more excited when the men showed them their new homes. In the shade of the blood-red flamboyant tree were three brand new thatched huts. Inside were gifts for each girl: a sweet straw bed, a cooking pot, a goat's hair blanket and two feather pillows. And a bed for the brother. The girls were delighted and that night everyone slept soundly in their new straw beds, fresh feather pillows beneath their heads.

When the girls awoke the next morning, their husbands were already up and ready to leave for the forest. 'Prepare, wives, for an enormous feast,' they said, waving goodbye, 'for we are off to hunt a delicious beast.' And indeed they did.

That night, the men returned with more meat than the girls had ever seen. Sitting round the fire, they feasted and laughed and feasted some more with their fine warrior husbands. Not one of them could quite believe how lucky she had been.

That day was no extraordinary day, though. Each day was as delightful, and each evening the men would return from their hunt with something equally delicious: a fat-bottomed kudu, a tender young zebra, a suckling wild piglet or a delicate duiker. The women ate and ate and ate and soon they became the fattest and strongest wives in the valley.

While the sisters were extremely content with their lives, their little brother was beginning to get suspicious. How did the three men manage to bring home so much meat? he wondered. How did their spears stay so clean and shiny? Why did they want his sisters to get so fat? And why did they never put on weight?

There was only one way to find out, he decided: to follow them. One day, as the men walked through the grass towards the forest, the little boy crept behind them, as stealthily as a leopard. Then, when they got to the forest, he hid behind a rock.

At first the men acted normally, chatting and collecting twigs to make a fire. But as soon as they'd made the fire everything changed. First they took off all their clothes. Then, when they were quite naked, they began to dance around the fire, pounding the earth with their feet, waving their arms and howling at the sky.

The boy watched, puzzled, from behind a rock. And the longer he watched, the bigger his eyes got. For, as the men whirled faster and faster round the fire, singing and whistling and yelling and stamping, their bodies began to sprout thick animal hair. Then tails shot out from their bottoms. And thick bushy manes grew from their necks. Before long the men no longer looked like men, but like three very large lions.

'So that is the secret of their hunting,' thought the terrified boy, as he lowered himself, trembling, behind the rock. 'They are lion men.'

Sure enough, soon the lions were roaring and prowling the forest, pouncing on animals for supper. When they had caught enough they returned to the fire, prowled round it until they turned back into men again, then set off home for supper.

The boy kept very quiet until the next morning, when he took his sisters aside and told them what he had seen. Of course they didn't believe anything he said. 'Nonsense, you silly little boy,' they scolded him. 'Our husbands might be as strong as lions, but they are certainly not wild animals. We don't know why you make up these stories.'

The boy was very upset that his sisters didn't believe him. 'I'll prove it to you,' he said. 'Just wait.' So when the warriors picked up their spears and went into the forest the next day, he followed them again. This time was even worse, for not only did he see the men turn into lions, but he overheard their conversation too. 'How many days do you think we'll have to wait until our little wifely beauties are fat enough to eat?' growled one lion to another. 'A day or two?' purred the second. 'Or perhaps tonight?' smirked the biggest one, slurping his lips. 'Mmmmmm, fresh, fat, female flesh!' the three lions roared.

'Oh no!' the brother thought, hiding behind a tree. 'They are going to eat my sisters!' Leaping up, he ran through the grass, over the rocks and into the village to warn his sisters that they were going to be supper. At first, he was so out of breath, he couldn't speak. But soon he was calm enough to blurt out his story. 'I promise you! The lion men will have you for supper! And if you don't believe me, come and look!' he shouted, dragging the reluctant women outside.

Sure enough, looking out towards the forest the sisters could see three enormous male lions walking towards them, growling and roaring, their eyes shining with hunger. The other villagers began to shout and beat their drums in warning. But the brother knew it wasn't the villagers the lions wanted. 'Follow me!' he shouted, leading his sisters to a tree. 'Quick, up here, unless you want to be lions' tea!'

For once the sisters obeyed their little brother, and at the top of the tree found an enormous flat reed basket that he had secretly made for their escape. 'Just jump in and drum the drum!' he shouted, as the drooling lions padded hungrily towards the tree. 'Quickly, drum!'

Luckily, although the sisters were rather heavy from all the food they had feasted on, the brother's magic basket worked a treat. No sooner had they climbed in and started to drum than the basket rose up into the sky, leaving the roaring lions behind. Soon the happy foursome were whizzing through the air, under the sun, past the clouds and back home to their village.

As the basket gently descended from the sky, the villagers raced out to see who had arrived. When the children's mother and father saw them, they almost cried with happiness – especially when they heard what their children's fate could have been. 'I thought I had taught you about strangers,' said their mother, sternly. 'Did I not tell you to beware of them – especially those promising gifts.'

'And there is another moral, Mother,' said the young boy proudly.

'Remember that the youngest is sometimes the wisest!' The sisters, for once, had to agree. For where would they be if their brother hadn't saved them? In three lions' tummies. For tea.

The lion and the jackal

Told to me in San by Nxo Kgimxou in XaiXai, Botswana

Once upon a time Jackal was walking along a path, looking, as usual, for a scrap of food to scrounge, when he came across a hungry looking lioness. 'Why are you so thin, Mrs Lion?' said Jackal, staring at his friend's bony body. Lioness looked at him with tears in her eyes. 'I am the unluckiest lioness in the world,' she said. 'I have no husband to protect me, no sisters to help me hunt, and no nanny to care for my five little cubs. In a drought like this, times are very tough.'

Jackal looked at her sympathetically. 'I know what you mean, Mrs Lion,' he said. 'I myself haven't had food for weeks, and am starving. Perhaps what we should do is work together. What about if you left your cubs with me every day to look after, and then you could hunt properly without worrying? I could be their nanny!'

Lioness was delighted with the idea and the next day she welcomed Jackal into her house. At first Jackal enjoyed living with a lion family. But after a few days of looking after five dusty cubs, cleaning the house and sweeping the yard while Lioness was out hunting, Jackal was exhausted. He was also very, very hungry. Lioness still hadn't managed to catch a single animal, and the cubs had had nothing to eat but their mother's milk. Slowly they were all starving.

One day when Lioness went out, the hungry Jackal looked at the five little cubs and had an idea. 'We haven't got food and there are five of you soft, tasty little things running around,' he said, looking at them wickedly. 'You, I'm afraid, will have to be stew!'

Quickly he pounced on one and within minutes had skinned it, chopped it and popped it into a pot to make a thick, meaty stew.

After scoffing a big bowl, he set aside a large plate of it for Lioness. 'These are, after all, her cubs we are cooking. It's only right she should get a share,' he said, smiling wickedly.

That night, when Lioness came home, she asked as usual about her cubs. 'I look after them so beautifully when you are away that they get fatter and happier by the day,' said Jackal. 'Now lie down here, Mother Lion, and I will get bring them over to you to suckle.' And off he trotted to the cubs' hut to get the first two cubs to drink from their mother. When the cubs tummies were rounded and full, Jackal took them back to their hut and collected the next two. Then it was the last cub's turn. This, of course, was a bit of a problem as it was in little bits in Jackal's stomach. So, Jackal just picked up the first one, and took it back to its mother for a second helping – something, luckily, Lioness didn't notice. Then, when the cubs were all in bed, Jackal presented her with a treat: a great big bowl of thick, steamy stew. Lion couldn't believe her luck. 'Where did you get this?' she said, with a happy slurp. 'Oh, from someone nearby,' said Jackal casually. 'Isn't it lucky for you that you have friends like me?' Lioness could not but agree.

The next day, when Lioness was gone, Jackal once again began to dream of lion cub stew. 'Mmmm, it was so delicious,' he sighed, remembering the thick brown gravy. 'So delicious, in fact, I think I will have to make another one.' Eyeing the fattest cub, he pounced again and stewed it.

At the end of the day, tired and hungry, Lioness returned to yet another wonderful supper – another gift from someone near, Jackal said. 'But tomorrow, Lioness, you are going to have to catch something when you go hunting,' said Jackal crossly. 'I can't be a husband and a wife to this family, finding food for us and tending the cubs. You have got to do something.' 'Yes, yes,' purred Lioness happily, chomping on a lovely soft stew bone. 'Tomorrow, I promise, dear friend Jackal we shall have kudu steak.' Then she lay down to suckle her cubs, as Jackal ran backwards and forwards with them, this time bringing two for second helpings to disguise the missing two who had been made into stew.

By the third day, Jackal had got quite used to his routine of catching a cub and cooking it. But he was getting worried about how many cubs were left, and what they would do when they ran out. 'What do you do in the bush all day?' he snapped at Lioness when she returned that night. 'I thought you were a hunter. Yet every day you return empty-pawed. When we run out of gifts, then what will we do?' 'I promise, tomorrow will be my lucky day, tomorrow,' said Lioness, flicking her tail happily in the air as she slurped delicious stew. 'And now, Mr Jackal, would you mind bringing me my cubs to suckle?'

Bringing the cubs to their mother was becoming tricky now there were only two left. But luckily, Jackal had an excuse. 'Your cubs are now so fat that I have to just bring them one by one,' he said, and, running backwards and forwards from the children's hut, he picked up one cub and dropped the other off, until Lioness thought she had suckled all five. 'I am so lucky to have you, Mr Jackal,' said Lioness contentedly. 'My cubs are fat, we are well fed, and our house is a happy one. If you were a lion, rather than a jackal, I would happily marry you.'

Jackal had now become immune to the fact that he was cooking cubs. In fact, he rather enjoyed it: taking off the soft skin, and stewing up the fatty flesh. Eating it was just as marvellous – very sweet and soft. But he knew that it wasn't going to last. With only one cub left, pretending to their mother there were five was going to be difficult. But, as usual, Jackal had his excuse ready when the last very fat, and very full, cub was carried backwards and forwards to its mother.

'I look after your cubs so well, Mrs Lioness, that they just don't need so much suckling at night,' he said soothingly. 'Just relax. They are very fat, and very contented. Lie down and have some stew.' So Mrs Lioness did just that, relaxing on the hut floor and slurping one of Mr Jackal's delicious suppers.

On the fifth day, Mr Jackal was more nervous than usual. There was only one cub left and if he cooked that, Mrs Lion was sure to be furious. 'What I'll have to do is eat it all myself,' he thought. So he did. He caught the lion cub, making it into the best stew he had ever made and he filled his tummy until he could eat no more. Then he ran up the hill overlooking the house, and spent the day snoozing.

At the end of the day, when Lioness returned, there was not a single thing to welcome her home: no Jackal, no supper and no babies. 'Mr Jackal, Mr Jackal, I'm home!' she roared, but no one came. She looked in the huts, but her babies were gone. She looked in the kitchen, but the stew pot was empty. And she looked in Mr Jackal's room, but all his things had vanished. It was outside, on the top of the hill above, that she spotted the smiling, fat-bellied jackal.

'Lioness, you have been a fool,' shouted Jackal from the hilltop. 'Did no one teach you that you should never leave your precious children with people you do not know? If you had not left your cubs with a stranger, this would never have happened. But instead you have eaten them every day for supper. And what tasty stew they were!'

Lioness gave a cry of rage and ran back into her children's hut, but Jackal was right. Her precious babies were gone. And under their beds lay five empty lion cub skins.

Lioness roared and howled all night, but it didn't help. She had lost her babies by entrusting them to a stranger. But she has never done it again since. Now, whenever she's hunting, Lioness leaves her cubswith her sister. And she keeps a watchful eye on Jackal. If you ever see the two animals in the grasslands today, notice how far apart they stay. Jackal is making sure Lioness can't get near enough to take revenge. And Lioness is making extra sure that Jackal goes nowhere near her babies.

The leper princess

Told to me in Bemba by Meka Lubemba at the
Latete leper colony in Zambia

Once upon a time a king decided it was time he got married. He had a
kingdom. He had a throne. But he had no wife or children. So he called
for his drummers. 'Drum throughout Africa,' he ordered, 'to tell the
people I want a queen. She must be strong and kind and beautiful. The
wedding will be held in one week.'

Soon the valleys were thronging with the sound of the king's drums
and girls up and down the land were dreaming of becoming queen. In
one village, three beautiful girls quickly prepared their bags for the
journey to meet the king. They packed sweet beeswax to soften their
feet, coconut oil to shine their skin, and soft cotton wraps fit for a
queen. Then they set off on the path towards the kingdom.

As they walked, they saw a shadow behind them. It was the village
leper. 'She's not coming with us,' they grumbled. 'We'll never be
accepted by a king if we are with a scabby leper.' So they picked up
sticks and started chasing the poor girl back.

A little way further the three girls saw an old woman sitting on the
side of the road. She was tired and dirty and dressed in rags. 'Please
kind girls would you help me?' the woman said. 'I am too old to get
water from the river and I am very thirsty. But I don't think I can
walk one step further.'

The girls shook their heads. 'Out of our way, Old Bag,' they said. 'We are on our way to marry the king. We have no time for old crones like you.' And off they walked. As they walked off, the leper girl came

creeping along the path behind them, careful to keep out of their way. When she got to the old lady she smiled. 'Hello, old lady,' she said, clapping her hands together respectfully. 'Are you all right?'

The old woman sighed. 'I am too old to get water from the river and I am very thirsty,' she said. The leper girl felt very sorry for the woman, so she sat her under a shady tree then took the woman's calabash and filled it with sweet, cold water from the river. The woman drank it thirstily before saying farewell. 'Bless you, sweet girl, and good luck,' the old woman said, and waved the girl goodbye.

The three girls were the first to arrive at the kingdom, and were shown by the elders to a beautiful hut. Inside were three beds, three bright woollen blankets, and a place for them to put their bags. The girls were very happy – it was perfect for them. Until, that is, they saw the leper girl arrive at the same door. 'Don't worry about her,' the girls said to the elders. 'She is a stupid, sick girl, and can sleep on the floor. If we leave the door open, perhaps a lion might even eat her in the night.'

As the leper girl lay miserably on the floor, the girls feasted and drank and danced at the king's house, until it was time to go to bed. Then they went back to their beds and soft blankets and dreamt of feasts and weddings.

Not everyone in the kingdom was asleep, though. During the night, the king's dreams had been interrupted by the voice of a wise old woman speaking to him. 'Find a girl with a peaceful face and she will be the queen of your dreams,' she had said.

Feeling that this voice was a prophecy, the king quietly stole out of his hut and crept around his village, looking at the sleeping faces of all the women. Some snored. Some sniffed. And some grunted. 'None of these will do,' the king sighed, creeping away.

Then he saw a hut with the door open. Quietly he tiptoed up to it and lying in the doorway, on the bare floor, he saw a girl with the most peaceful face he had ever seen. 'The old woman was right: a girl's heart is reflected in her face,' he thought. Without waking her, he gently picked her up and carried her back to his palace.

In the morning, the three beautiful girls woke up and looked at the floor. 'Hurrah!' they shouted. 'The lion has had supper. He has come in at night and stolen the leper girl!' They danced around the room and celebrated, for the scabby leper girl was gone. Their way was now clear to enchant the king.

But just as they had put on their beautiful new clothes, and rubbed oil into their skins, the drums started to beat. 'All come outside, All come outside, It's time to celebrate, our king has a bride!' said the drums. The girls looked at each other in horror, then ran into the sunlight.

Sure enough, beside the king on a carved wooden throne, sat the leper girl. But instead of a sick, scabby girl, there sat a beautiful lady, with the softest skin, the widest smile, the whitest teeth and the kindest face anyone had ever seen. 'Warriors, elders and people of my kingdom,' said the king. 'I present to you my queen.'

The girls gasped. As they stared, with their mouths hanging open, an old lady came up to them – the old lady they had passed on the pathway. 'Remember, girls, that goodness is always rewarded,' she said. 'And a good person's heart is always reflected in her face – even if it is temporarily scarred by sores.'

The three girls walked home quietly, thinking of the lesson they had learnt. And the queen celebrated in her new home – beside the king in the palace of the great kingdom.

The leopard's promise

Told to me in Tonga by Mafuta Siabwanda, a builder in Bulawayo, and in Shona by Justice Chinamhora in Harare, Zimbabwe

One day Leopard was dragging home an antelope for his supper when he fell into a big, black pit made by a man.

Leopard felt very sorry for himself. The pit was deep and dark and cold and his body was battered and bruised from the fall. What was he going to do? he panicked. How was he going to get out? Then from above he heard a laugh. It was Hyena! 'Help! Help, Hyena!' roared Leopard from trap. 'I have fallen in a pit. Please help me.'

But Hyena was in no mood to help Leopard. 'What do you do for me?' he howled. 'You always call me a scavenger, so I am going to do just that. I am going to take your antelope and enjoy it in peace. Goodbye!' Then off he trotted.

The furious leopard wasn't left alone long, though. The path the man had dug the pit in was used by most jungle animals, and soon Leopard had all sort of animals peering over the edge. First the baboons sauntered by, then the warthogs. The birds flew in and the giraffe peered in. But not a single one would lend a hand. Leopard had killed too many of their friends for his supper.

One day passed, then another. Just as Leopard was getting desperate, a man walked by. 'Please, kind Man, help me out of here,' whimpered Leopard. 'I am thirsty and hungry, and if you don't help me, I will die. Please hear my cry!'

The man looked sympathetically at the Leopard. He was indeed thin. And he did look bruised and tired. 'If I let you out, Leopard, you have to promise one thing,' he said, staring Leopard in the eye. 'You cannot catch me or eat me. And you will leave Man alone for ever more.'

Leopard, desperate to get out of the pit, nodded his head. 'I promise,' he purred, 'I promise!' So the man nervously lowered his hand, held on to Leopard's paw and hauled him from the deep, dark pit. But as soon as he was on firm ground, Leopard's eyes sparkled and mouth watered. 'Hurrah, supper!' he snarled hungrily at the man. 'I never thought I would find food so fast!'

The man's body shook with terror. 'You promised, Leopard,' he quivered, 'that you would never eat me or another man again. You promised!'

But Leopard growled grumpily. 'That was then and this is now, you silly man!' he said. 'Wait until I have sharpened my claws!'

The man was desperate. He looked round for help, but there was no one about. The only thing nearby was the river. 'River, river, help me!' he shouted, 'Leopard wants to eat me for tea!'

But the river just ambled by. 'Why should I help you, Man?' it gurgled. 'You wash your dirty clothes in me, swim in me and drink me. What have you ever done to help me?' The man sighed. He knew the river was right.

So he turned to the trees. 'Trees, trees, come and help me,' he begged. 'The Leopard wants to eat me for tea!' But the trees, too, turned their leaves away. 'We shade you, let your children climb us, and all you do is burn us!' they rustled in the wind. 'When you learn to help us, we'll help you, Man.'

In desperation, the man turned to Hare, who was hopping along the path. 'Hare, please help me,' he begged. 'Leopard promised not to harm me, but now he wants to eat me for tea.'

The hare turned to the leopard. 'Is this true?' he asked, looking sternly at the big cat. 'Yes it is,' growled Leopard, sizing up the appetising hare. 'But why should I not eat this man? His brothers are the ones who dug the pit. His fathers are the ones who spear my family. And his sisters are the ones who shout at me if I visit their village. What's a promise if Man has only ever harmed me?'

'I see,' said Hare thoughtfully. 'This is rather complicated. And I am not sure I follow it all. If you don't mind, kind Leopard, I would like you to go back to the very beginning and show me exactly what happened. Once I've seen it with my own eyes, at least I can judge whether you should eat the man for tea.'

Wanting food as quickly as possible, Leopard agreed. Just as Hare had asked, he leapt down the pit again, and started to relate the story – of how Hyena had refused to rescue him, and the baboons, and the birds, and even Warthog. Then he got to the part when Man came along.

'Please will you help me out Man?' he said again, staring out of the pit at the hare and the man. This time, though, what do you think the man answered.

'I trusted you once, but I won't do it again, you foolish Leopard. A liar like you deserves to stay in a deep, dark pit. And a friendly, helpful man like me deserves to go home with his friend Hare for tea. Goodbye.'

And off the man went, pondering the lessons he had learnt that day. From then on, he only cut trees that were old and dying so that the trees would be his friends. He washed his clothes in a bowl, so the river would respect him again. He stopped trapping hares in snares, for it was the wise little long-eared creature which had helped him escape. And he never, ever trusted a leopard again. His mother had always told him that a leopard never changes its spots – that a hungry leopard will always be a hungry leopard no matter how many promises it makes. But until that day he hadn't known what she meant. Now he did – and he never forgot it.

The leopard and the dog

Told to me in Bemba by Christina Mumba on the Kalamazi rose farm outside Lusaka, Zambia

A long time ago, when the earth was young, Leopard and Dog were great friends. Every day the two of them would walk in the tall grasses together, hunt hares, sip cool water from the river and sit in the evening sharing a delicious meal of duiker, rabbit, or bushpig – whatever they had caught that day. Wherever Dog went, Leopard went. And vice versa.

One day, Leopard decided he wanted to marry. He'd been a bachelor long enough, he said, and wanted a mate to have cubs with. So, he packed his little bag, waved goodbye to Dog and set off on a journey to find a bride.

A few weeks later, Leopard was back, looking very pleased with himself. Not only had he met a beautiful girl who he loved with all his heart, he told Dog, but her father had agreed to let them marry. All he had to do was go back to pay the bride's father lobola (the price all bridegrooms must pay for a bride's hand) and discuss the details of the wedding. Then he'd have his own wife.

The next few days the two friends gathered together gifts that would impress the bride's father. Dog poured some strong, fresh beer into a pumpkin calabash. Leopard knocked down ripe figs from the tree. Then the pair of them raided the termites' nest for the sweetest, softest, whitest termites they could find – a treat no one could resist.

On the day of their journey, the two animals got up before dawn, and made sure they were handsome enough to meet a bride. While the vain Leopard licked and picked and flicked his fur until it glowed golden in the dawn light, Dog loaded their gifts into a little bag on his back. Then the friends set off on the long wedding journey.

At first the air was cool, and the paths soft and well shaded. But by noon, when the sun was high in the sky, both animals were exhausted. 'Let's sing,' suggested Leopard, purring a tune to himself. 'I know a great song that would put a spring in our steps!' And he started to sing, waving his hips in time to the tune as he padded along. 'Bonyoro kenda, bonyoro kenda nogoro ya ngui.' And again: 'Bonyoro kenda, bonyoro kenda nogoro ya ngui.'

Rather than lift Dog's spirits, though, the song made him very upset. 'When the dog was created, God made a mistake, because his bottom waddles like that of a goose!' he thought indignantly. 'How dare Leopard insult me so much! How dare he!'

As he walked along, trying to think of his own song that might pay Leopard back, Dog got crosser and crosser. 'Some friend!' he sulked.

'I think I'm going to have to teach him a lesson. All this talk of beautiful brides has made him far too big for his paws.'

When they got to a thicket of dense green bushes, Dog called out to the sniggering, singing Leopard. 'My dear friend, Leopard,' he said pleasantly. 'Please do excuse me a second. I must do some urgent business here – I won't be long.' And off he dashed into the thicket.

Out of the sight of Leopard, Dog quickly slung the gifts from his back, and took out the bag of termites. 'Bow, wow, wow!' he giggled, wagging his tail in excitement. 'This trick will surely pay that sniggering Leopard back.'

After putting a small portion of termites aside, Dog then set about eating every single termite in the bag, delicious mouthful after delicious mouthful, until he felt quite sick. Then in one quick motion, he vomited them all up back into the bag – every single ant. 'A terrible waste,' Dog sighed, surveying the bag of nasty-smelling sick. 'But oh! What sweet revenge!' He then took the little portion of live termites that he had put aside on the top of the thick, sticky mess to disguise it, put the bag back on his back and went again to join Leopard.

On the journey, Leopard continued to sing his insulting song, howling louder and louder as they went, smugly thinking that Dog was too stupid to understand it. Dogs, as you know, are very clever, and this one not only understood it, but had already planned his revenge. 'Just wait, you pompous cat, just you wait,' growled Dog to himself. 'You'll be sorry.'

At sunset, when the pair arrived at the village, the bride's family excitedly gathered round to welcome their guests. Leopard was a fine prospective husband, they all agreed, with his spotted golden coat, sharp white teeth and fine hunting claws. Soon they were all chatting round the fire, planning dances and feasts and wedding celebrations.

While Leopard showed off round the fire, boasting to his new family of the great kills he had made, the kudu he had eaten, and the great mountains he had climbed, Dog quietly laid the termite bag near the fire, and crept off into the darkness.

Soon it was supper time, but when the hosts came to give Dog some of the celebratory feast, he wasn't there. No matter how hard they called or how shrilly they whistled, he was gone.

Leopard wasn't worried about his friend at all. In fact, he was rather enjoying the tribe's undivided attention. 'Don't worry about Dog,' he said, in that smooth voice that leopards have. 'He'll be back, he'll be back. Now, about that kudu I was telling you …'

After a feast of stew and maize meal and several horns of beer, it was time, the elders of the tribe decided, to bring out Leopard's gifts. A young boy was summoned to bring the bag over, and at once the father of the bride started to open it. As he did so, his eyes glowed. 'Figs! And beer! And termites!' he exclaimed, obviously delighted with the big bag of treats. 'Bring me some baskets – pudding has begun!'

Two long baskets were brought for the termite feast, and a boy gently started to take out the sweet, white creatures with his fingers. But after some real termites, a fetid yellow substance started to stick to his hands, and something disgusting flowed from the bag – something thick, and sticky, and very smelly. Something that looked remarkably like dog sick.

The elders of the tribe were furious. 'You woo our precious bride, you eat our food, you drink our beer – and what do you bring us?' they shouted angrily at Leopard, waving their spears in the firelight. 'Shame, Leopard, shame! This is a very sick joke. Be gone! We will never forget this. From now on, you will be our enemy!'

As the warriors' shouts turned louder and louder, the terrified leopard leapt up and, with his tail between his legs, ran off into the dark night. Being far too embarrassed to go home in such disgrace without a wife, he sadly padded off into the hills. He has lived there alone ever since, far away from Man and Dog, only ever coming out at night. And Dog, being a clever kind of creature, now lives with Man, for he knows that wherever he goes, Leopard will be on the lookout for him.

The incredible Mr Tortoise

Told to me in Bemba by a leper, Costa
Chibilikita, at the Latete leper colony in Zambia
and in Bemba by David Siame in Fringilla,
Zambia

There was a time when, although Tortoise was very small, he had a very high opinion of himself. 'I am the strongest creature in the kingdom,' he would boast to whoever would listen. 'No one else in the jungle is as powerful as me.'

In the beginning, most animals just ignored the little creature's idle boasts. But soon the big boys began to get irritated – especially Elephant and Hippo, who, as we all know, are the strongest animals in the jungle. 'How could such a weak little creature think he is as powerful as us?' they harrumphed. 'Who does that scaly little longnecked shell think he is?' And off they snorted, and stamped and trumpeted, just to prove to the jungle what big fellows they were.

The little Quelea, who was a nosy little bird with a red bill, heard the earth shake and the trees fall as the big boys stomped about, and immediately flew off to warn Tortoise. 'I would keep right out of the way of Elephant and Hippo,' he chirruped and chirped, hopping in the trees about Tortoise's head. 'They're in a bad mood, Tortoise, and if you don't watch it, they'll squash you flat with one of their big flat front feet.'

But Tortoise just smiled to himself. 'I'll show them all,' he said, a wide smile breaking out on his brown scaly face. 'I will show them what strength is.'

First thing the next morning, Tortoise stretched his long head and legs out of his shell, nibbled on a bit of dewy grass for breakfast, and started the long trundle to find Elephant. It took a while, as tortoises aren't the speediest of creatures, but at last he found the mighty Elephant nibbling fresh acacia leaves in the forest.

'Greetings Mr Elephant,' he shouted up in the loudest voice he could muster. 'If you don't mind, I want to talk to you.' Elephant couldn't believe his big grey ears. 'You want to talk to me!' he trumpeted at the little creature in astonishment. 'Why, yes, in fact I do, Mr Elephant. I think we have something to discuss. A little bird told me that you believe I am not as strong as you. And I think you are wrong. In fact, I believe that equals like us should stick together and be friends.'

Elephant was so taken aback by the creature's cheek that soon he began to see the funny side. 'You! Mr Tortoise! You think you are as strong as the rock of the jungle?' he cried, rocking with laughter. 'And how are you going to prove that, you skinny-legged reptile?'

'Well,' said Tortoise, a bit put out. 'I thought that perhaps we might have a tug of war. If either of us can pull the other from his place, he is the most powerful. If neither of us can manage it, we must agree that we are equals.'

Elephant thought it was rather a foolish idea. As everyone knew, he could pull Tortoise into the air with just one tug. But, to settle the matter, he agreed. 'Right, tomorrow it is,' he said, as Tortoise handed him the end of a very long vine. 'But you'd better hold on tight to your end, Tortoise, for tomorrow I am going to make you fly!'

Tortoise then set off to see Hippo, who was cooling off in a shallow pool. 'Hello Mr Hippo,' he said, as Hippo opened one eye above the water. 'I was just wondering whether you could help out with something. Would you agree that I am stronger than you?' Hippo thought he was hearing things. 'How can you think you are as strong as I, the Water Cow?' he snorted furiously, blowing big bubbles from his nose. 'Get away, you silly creature, before I toss you into the air with one of my teeth!' With that, he gave a grunt, and disappeared crossly underwater.

Ten minutes later, when Hippo surfaced again, Tortoise was still there. He couldn't believe the little creature's cheek. 'Are you deaf as well as stupid?' grunted Hippo with a nasty glint in his eye. 'Which part of "go away" do you not understand?'

'Well,' said Tortoise, marching up to the river creature, his head held high. 'It's just that the rest of the animals have all agreed with me that I am stronger than you. And I just thought it would be a good chance for you to prove them wrong. But if you don't want to, fine!' And off he stamped.

Hippo couldn't believe his stumpy little ears. How could the animals believe that that timid Tortoise was stronger than him? So he called Tortoise back. 'If that's how you want it, fine!' he snorted. 'But I'm warning you, Tortoise: I am still going to toss you into the air with my teeth once I have pulled you over here.' Timidly, Tortoise gave him his end of the vine and agreed that tomorrow, when Tortoise tugged on his end of the vine, Hippo would tug too.

Early the next morning Tortoise went to the centre of the vine and started to shake it. And, just as he had predicted, Elephant began to pull on his end. Then five seconds later Hippo started. Tortoise was delighted. 'My trick has worked, my trick has worked! What a clever Tortoise I am!' he sang, waving his stumpy legs in the air. 'Now we'll see what strength is.'

All day the two enormous animals pulled. As morning turned to afternoon, they got increasingly tired and sweaty. But neither would give up. Elephant pulled and puffed, as the vine twisted round his stretching trunk. And Hippo heaved and huffed, tugging hard on the vine twisted around his tooth. But neither would consider letting Tortoise win.

After a while, Tortoise began to feel sorry for the beasts. It was a hot day and they must both be exhausted. So, taking a knife, he walked to the centre of the vine and, with a little slash, cut it in two. From one end of the jungle came an almighty crash. And from the other end, rose an almighty splash. Oh, how hard those animals must have fallen, he giggled.

Running as fast as his little legs would take him Tortoise went first to visit Elephant, who had fallen on his back, his trunk twisted and blue from pulling so hard. 'Why Tortoise,' Elephant whimpered, as he tried to raise his great, grey body off the ground. 'I had no idea you were as strong as you are. I apologise for my rudeness. From now on, consider yourself my equal.' And he put out his battered trunk in friendship.

Tortoise shook his trunk happily, then marched over to the pool to see Hippo. Usually the creature was lazily poking an eye out of the water, but this time, he was floating on its surface, exhausted, with one of his huge teeth missing. 'My thear Thorthoise,' said Hippo, lisping through the gap where his tooth was. 'I am tho thorry I was tho rude. Pleath leths be frienths.' And he slowly swam out to offer a fat paw to Tortoise.

Tortoise, of course, was delighted his trick had worked and, congratulating himself on his powers, he marched off into the jungle as the word spread about his incredible powers. He has never had a day's trouble from any beast of the jungle. But if you ask him how he did it he has only one thing to say: 'Strength is not in the arm, but in the head, dear creatures. In the head.' And he's right. Often in life it is not the strength of a creature's brawn that matters. It is the cunning of his brain.

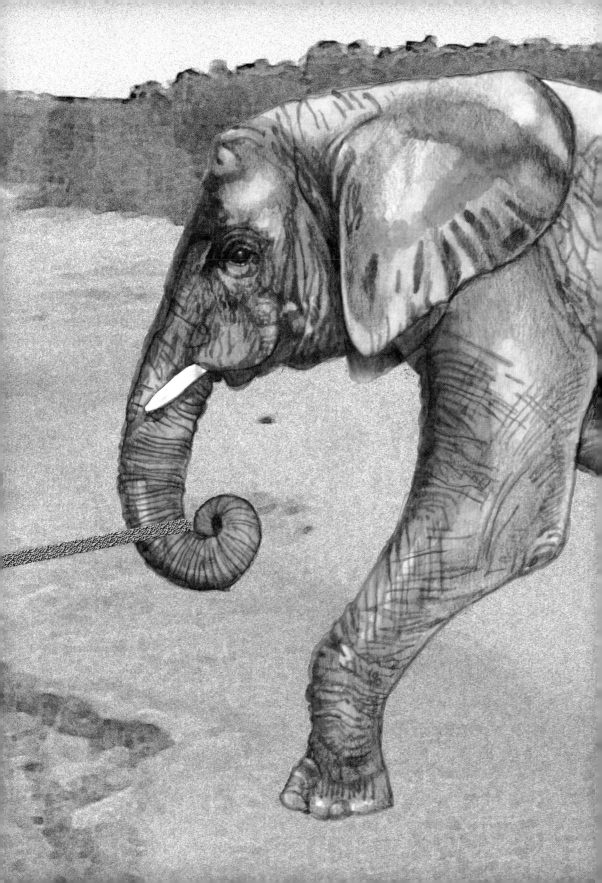

The Hen's safari

Told to me in Shona by Sabina Sinjere in Mabvuku, Zimbabwe

Hen, the fattest of the kraal chickens, was bored. Her life was always the same, she sighed: scratching at dry red soil, peck-peck-pecking at corn seeds, flapping around her little yellow chicks and putting up with the loud, bumptious cock-a-doodle-doing of her bossy old husband, the kraal rooster. What she needed was an adventure. 'Today,' she decided, 'I am going to take myself off on safari. It's about time I escaped this kraal and saw the world.'

So one afternoon after she'd tucked her little chicks up for their nap under a nearby acacia tree, she evaded the sharp eye of her rooster husband, and giving her feathers a quick powdering in the soft rusty dust by the chief's hut, Hen set off down the kraal path towards the river. The riverbank, according to her friend, Goat, was brimming with exotic creatures: kingfishers with emerald wings, silver fish that could leap over rocks, and beetles that could roll dung balls bigger than their own bodies. This was going to be a day that the kraal hen would never forget!

Hen set out full of the joys of Africa. The sun had turned the afternoon golden with its rays, the msasa trees gently shaded her with their limy leaves, and soon she could smell the weedy, watery, willowy, wet wafts of the river in the wind.

Hen had never been on safari, so once she'd got to the riverbank, she wasn't quite sure what to do. 'I know – I'll have a drink,' she clucked, scuttling her plump body down to the water.

It all seemed so peaceful, with the river flowing gently by, Mr Kingfisher sitting on a dry branch watching out for fish, and the sun gently glimmering on the water. The only thing that moved in the midday sun was a log gently floating by.

Because she was a village bird, Hen had no idea that the log floating by was not a log at all, but a well-disguised and very hungry crocodile, who couldn't believe his luck having such a delicious dinner delivered right to his riverbank. And as Hen happily sipped away at her first safari drink of the day, the hungry crocodile swam quietly towards the bank, then sprang from the water, snapping up Hen in one big snap!

'Oh Brother!' squawked Hen, her scrawny neck sticking out of a big gap in Crocodile's brown, rotting teeth. 'I beg of you, Brother, please don't!'

Crocodile was so shocked on hearing Hen refer to him as brother that his mouth flew open, leaving Hen to flap out on to the riverbank. 'Brother?' he said, not quite believing that he had let his supper go. 'How on earth can I be Hen's brother?'

As Hen wandered along the riverbank, covered in chickenbumps from shock, Crocodile had another think. Not only was his belly rumbling and his mouth salivating from the thought of chicken dinner, but one of Hen's feathers was still stuck between his teeth, making him look extremely silly. 'I have been tricked by a stupid town bird,' he grumbled. 'This time I cannot let her escape!' So, creeping up behind her, he snapped her up in his jaws. But again, Hen let out a bloodcurdling squawk. 'Brother, oh Brother,' she squealed, 'Release me, don't eat me!' Hearing those words, and not wanting to eat a sister, Crocodile let her go.

Crocodile was so shocked by his own actions that he decided to go and seek advice from the Great River God. On his way he saw his equally scaly friend, Lizard, cooling his slippery white tummy on some moss. 'Where are you off to in such a hurry?' hissed Lizard.

'Oh Lizard, I am in a terrible tizz,' said Crocodile, sliding on to a warm rock. 'There was a lovely kraal-bred hen who I caught twice, but I just had to let go because every time her lovely feathered flesh touched my tongue, she squawked out 'Oh Brother!' Of course, Lizard, I can't eat my own sister! So now I am off to the water spirit to talk it over.'

'Don't bother,' said the lazy lizard, flicking his tongue languidly to catch a passing dragonfly. 'Don't you see, dear Crocodile, that Duck lives near the water and she lays eggs. Turtle lives near the water and she lays eggs. I live in water, and I lay eggs. So do you. We are all brothers of a type. And none of us eats the other.'

'So we are,' thought Crocodile, slinking back into the cool depths. 'I think I will go and catch something else for supper. Something that doesn't lay eggs.'

From that day on, crocodiles have preferred eating mammals, such as buffaloes or zebras. And hens have rarely gone on safari again.

The hawk and the hen

Told to me in Shona by Isaac Cherenje in Harare, Zimbabwe

Long ago, Hawk and Hen were very good friends. Hen roosted in a kraal with her seven chicks, and Hawk nested on the peak of a high mountain. But although they lived far apart, they still behaved like neighbours, helping each other with favours, food or even feathers whenever the other needed it.

One day, when Hen noticed how straggly her chicks were looking, the first friend she turned to for help was Hawk. 'Dear Hawk,' she called to her friend up the mountain, 'please may I borrow that marvellous razor you found glinting on a hill? My little chicks are looking so ugly and untidy, with their long, unkept feathers. They desperately need a trim.'

Hawk could not refuse Hen, knowing that his neighbour often gave him an egg or two to eat, or a glossy feather for his nest, so he was happy to fly down his precious tool for her to borrow. There was one condition, though. 'I simply must have it back tomorrow, if you don't mind, Hen,' said Hawk, 'because lots of other birds borrow that razor from me. Of course, I won't charge you a fee to use it, but I must have it back or there will be a queue of birds complaining.'

Hen was very grateful to Hawk for the loan, and as soon as she got home, she gathered up her bedraggled chicks. One by one she trimmed their dusty farmyard feathers until they looked perfectly round, golden and fluffy again. When she had finished, she marched

the sharp razor over to the henhouse, and put it safely on a high shelf where no small feet could step on it.

Once the razor was out of sight, Hen completely forgot about it, continuing her days as normal – scratching for food, nesting in the soft grass, and clucking over her chicks. It was only four days later, when a great Hawk's shadow fell over the kraalyard, that she suddenly remembered her promise. 'I do wish you'd get a brain, Hen,' Hawk chided crossly.

Hen was mortified. 'Dear friend Hawk,' she clucked in a great fluster, wings flapping and feathers flying. 'I put your precious razor in such a high, safe place in the henhouse that I clean forgot about it. Please forgive me. I'll get it now.'

Hen flew into the henhouse, and with a squawk, flapped up onto the shelf shelf. But where she had put the silver shiny tool, there was a space. The razor had gone. Imagining the look on Hawk's face when he found out, Hen frantically looked around the kraal. She scratched around on the floor, but it wasn't there. She peered her beady eye under the children's nest, but it wasn't there either. She searched the firestones, in the store, by the water trough, under the maize tray, but it was nowhere to be found. Hawk's precious tool had simply vanished.

When Hen shamefacedly shuffled out into the kraal to break the bad news, Hawk was furious. 'Mine was the only razor in the bird kingdom,' he snapped, his yellow eyes flashing wildly. 'There is no substitute. It must be returned, Hen. I will give you one more day, then you'll have to pay!' With that, he gave a mighty flap, lifted his huge yellow claws off the earth, and with a piercing cry, swept off into the night.

Poor Hen spent all night searching, but found nothing. She demolished her henhouse, searched the straw, picked about in the rubble of the walls, in the ashes of the fire, and even in the rubbish. But she found nothing.

The next day, as promised, Hawk returned as Hen was looking through a heap of long grass. 'As a neighbour and friend,' said Hawk, staring at Hen in the eye, 'I have been very good to you. But I'm afraid this time I must be compensated. In payment, I am going to take a chick for my supper. And tomorrow I will be back.' Hen was very upset to lose one of her chicks, but Hawk was such a powerful bird, with such big, sharp claws and razor beak, that she couldn't refuse. 'I'll be back,' he snapped, flying away with a squeaking chick clutched to his breast. 'I will be back.'

True to his word, the next evening he returned. And despite Hen's clucking and flapping and scratching and biting, he took another chick. The same has been happening every day until today. That is the reason why, when you see a hen, she is always scratching on the ground. And a hawk is always circling, looking for its payment of a baby chick.

The greedy spider

Told to me in Nyemba by Madeleine Chisala in Lusaka, Zambia

Once upon a time, Spider lived with his wife and children in a village. He was a very greedy spider, and ate everything he came across. If he saw a fly passing by he'd pounce and catch it. If he chanced upon a fat worm, he'd slip it slyly into his mouth. And if he got an opportunity to steal a delicious bite of fruit from someone else's fields, he would. He was the craftiest food-finder about.

The problem was that Spider hated to share. Every day as he ploughed and hoed his fields, he thought of ways to sneak a snack so no one else would see it – or have to share it. He'd chomp a mosquito here and steal a fruit there. Soon he became so good at it that his abdomen became heavy and bloated.

Mrs Spider couldn't understand it. She was a mere slip of a woman, with similarly tiny children. How could her husband be so fat, she wondered.

One day, her husband came home with an answer. 'I am sorry to tell you, dear wife,' he said, holding his bloated body with his hands, 'but I am about to die.'

While Mrs Spider began to cry, Spider didn't seem upset at all. In fact, he seemed rather jolly. 'I have had a message from the heavens,' he said, smiling, 'as long as I am buried near our crops in a large coffin with the instruments I need, life will be marvellous. Apparently I will need gardening tools, salt, water, matches and cooking oil where I am going, so I would be grateful if you would prepare them. Oh, and whatever you do, don't put soil on top of my coffin.'

The next day, the puzzled Mrs Spider set about doing as her husband had ordered. She found a large coffin, some matches, gardening tools, salt, a bottle of water and a container of cooking oil, and, puffing and panting, she dragged them all home. When she got inside, there lay Mr Spider on the floor, dead.

Mrs Spider was very upset. But, knowing how happy her husband was about dying, she picked him up, put him into his large, airy coffin with his food, matches and tools and that afternoon, she and her children buried him in his favourite field. Then they went home sadly to sleep.

With Mr Spider gone, it was up to Mrs Spider to go to the field and pick crops for the family's dinner. Every day, she took her basket to select fine sorghum, gather fat flies, and pick a perfect pumpkin. But one day she arrived and half of her crops were gone! Her peppers had been pinched, her sorghum stolen, her tomatoes taken and even her pawpaws picked. And because the thief had taken her fruit, there was not a single wiggly worm or fat fly to be found.

As soon as she got back to their village, Mrs Spider reported the theft to the chief. 'My husband has only been gone a week, and some nasty creature has filched our food,' wept Mrs Spider. The Chief was suitably supportive and promised that night he would send a group to guard the field. 'Even if he's a silent as a ghost, we'll catch him, Mrs Spider,' he promised.

That night, as the chief said, a group of fearsome creatures gathered in the maize to watch over Mrs Spider's fields. Dung Beetle stood guard, showing off his strong front pinchers. Scorpion loaded his tail with painful poison. Snake sharpened his fangs. And Wasp prepared his sting.

By the light of the moon, the creatures stood and watched. At first nothing happened. But soon, as they peered through the maize, they saw the strangest sight they had ever seen – a creature covered in leaves coming out of Mr Spider's grave. It looked like a walking plant.

'What's that?' said Scorpion, his tail flicking ferociously into the air. But no one knew. As they watched, the creature sat down and made a fire. Then it took some vegetables out of Mr Spider's grave and started to cook.

'Ghosts can't cook, so it can't be a ghost,' hissed Snake. 'Leaves don't make fires, so it can't be a leaf,' whispered Wasp. 'No nice person keeps his food in a grave, so it must be a naughty thief!' stuttered Scorpion. 'Let's get him!'

The creatures stormed out of the crops, hitting and stinging and flicking the thief. But their punishment didn't last long. For as soon as the creature began to yell in pain, they recognised his voice. It was Mr Spider!

'Mr Spider, we thought you were dead!' squeaked Dung Beetle. 'We buried you a week ago!' whispered Wasp. 'Please tell me you're not a ghost!' wept Mrs Spider.

But he wasn't a ghost. As Mr Spider later admitted to the Chief, he was a terrible trickster. He had pretended to die so he could be buried in his favourite field of food. That way, when no one was watching, he could climb out and eat as much as he liked. Without asking anyone. And without sharing.

The creatures all agreed that no one had ever been such a mean husband. Or such a rotten liar. As punishment, the chief ordered Mr Spider to spend his life in a corner, with his back to the world. No one would ever talk to him again.

That's why, still today, most daddy long-legs spiders spend their lives by themselves in corners. It is punishment for their greed and for pretending to be dead.

The forbidden fruit

Told to me in Ndebele by Benicah Ncube in Bulawayo, Zimbabwe

Once upon a time there was a fruit that grew only at the very top of a tall mountain in the south of Africa. The fruit hung, ripe and rich and red, from the branch of a tall tree, and from the forest in the valley below, all the animals could see it. But none of them had ever tasted the fruit, because the mountain was too steep for them to climb.

The animals all looked up longingly at the red fruit, imagining its sweet, succulent taste. And the more they looked at it, the more they wanted it.

One day they could stand the temptation no longer, so the king called a meeting to decide how to get a taste of the forbidden fruit. Hare was the first to speak up. 'Being a great jumper, I could reach the fruit easily,' he said (in that smug way that hares do). 'But I might not be able to resist taking the first bite of it. I think we need someone trustworthy. Why don't we ask Tortoise first?'

The animals all thought this was a very good idea. 'He's slow, but he's steady and honest,' they agreed. So the next day Tortoise was dispatched, up the path, over the river, and step by precarious step, up the slippery slopes of the mountain. He climbed, and struggled and slid. But halfway up, the cliff was too much for his flat, scaly feet to hold on to and he flipped onto his back, and slid all the way back down into the forest on his hard shell.

The slope, it was agreed, was obviously too great for such a small creature to try. So, after helping Tortoise back onto his feet, they asked Kudu to try next. 'Please Mr Kudu,' they begged, 'make the leap into the land of the fruit tree, and bring a taste of the forbidden fruit.' With a toss of his curly horns, Kudu trotted off, and was soon high on the slopes. But he too failed, for no sooner had his hard hooves touched the slippery rocks than he began to stumble and eventually tumble - a mass of flying hooves and hair, off the mountain slope and into the jungle.

Baboon tried the next day – and fell when the cliff face began to crumble. So Hare came to the conclusion he should indeed try himself. He said to the other animals: 'I am sure of foot and nimble of paw, I am as sharp of brain as I am of claw.' And that, the confident creature felt, was reason enough to be the one to pursue the pleasures of the forbidden fruit.

Hare was right in one way. Unlike the other animals, his route didn't go up the path, over the river and up the slope. That was far too difficult, he decided. Instead, it went around the less steep slopes of the mountain, and up to the top. It was simple, and by sunset, the big-headed animal was back in the forest, triumphantly calling the others to see the rich, red, ripe fruit he held in his paw.

There was great excitement as they gathered, with everyone jostling and pushing and shoving to get near it. The fruit not only looked irresistible, but its fragrance was the sweetest anyone had ever smelt – mango and honey and strawberry all rolled into one.

They all wanted to try it, and soon a riot had begun. 'I'm the biggest, so I should be the first to tickle my tastebuds,' trumpeted Elephant, heaving forward. 'Stuff and Nonsense! Make way for the monarch!' roared Lion, flicking his tail. 'Hold on, hold on – what about me!' snorted the Hippo, flaring her nostrils.

It was all going precisely as Hare had planned. While the animals rattled and roared, and harrumphed and hawwed, the clever little creature put the forbidden fruit under his arm and slipped off into his burrow for a private feast.

The rest of the animals have still never tasted the forbidden fruit. If you see them now near a mountain, watch and see. They will still be looking up trying to spot another tree.

The fish's heads

Told to me in Chichewa by Evalena Njovu at the Latete leper colony in Zambia

A long time ago there lived two brothers, Mabvuko and Masoka. Mabvuko was a rich man with a beautiful house, and many servants. But greed had made him mean and arrogant, and no one liked him. Masoka, however, was the most generous, kind man in the land, always sharing whatever he had. If he caught three fish, he would give away two. If he found a mango tree bulging with fruit, he would call the other villagers to feast. If he came upon a sweet stream in the mountains, he would fill his pot so he could share it on the way home.

One night, Masoka dreamt that while he was sleeping on his mat under a tree, a beautiful girl called out to him. 'Come to the river,' she sang sweetly, 'Come and see what the Gods have given to thee.' Once he reached the river, the beautiful girl clapped three times and from the depths of the murky water rose the finest canoe he had ever seen. Three more claps produced paddles. Then the beautiful girl said to him, 'Now, Masoka, go and gather me some fish. When you bring them back, though, be sure to cut the heads off.' He did as he was commanded, and when he got back with the headless fish, the beautiful girl cooked them for him, then kissed him on his forehead.

When he woke up the next morning, Masoka was very disappointed to find it was all a dream. 'Never mind,' he sighed, picking up his fishing rod and heading for the river. 'I do not have my Dream Girl, but perhaps I will catch a fish.'

When he arrived at the river, Masoka was amazed to find not only the beautiful canoe he had dreamt of, but a pair of fine wooden paddles. Joyfully, he leapt inside and paddled out to the middle of the lake, where he caught the biggest fish of his life. Mindful of his dream, though, he cut off its head, before heading back home to cook it for lunch.

Imagine Masoka's amazement when he found in place of his old mat a fine thatched house, with carved wooden furniture, nine servants who bowed down before him, and, on the verandah, his Dream Girl who came out to greet him. She had been sent by God, she explained, to reward Masoka for his kindness and generosity, and to console and comfort him. Never again would he be lonely, hungry or thirsty. The only thing he had to promise, she reminded him, was never to bring home fish with their heads still attached.

Masoka had never been so happy. Every day he laughed with his Dream Girl, fished in his canoe, had his dinner cooked by servants,

and went to bed in his beautiful house. His rich brother, Mabvuko, even came to visit to witness his brother's sudden wealth.

Soon, though, Masoka began to tire of cutting off the fish heads. Why did his servants have to clean and behead them at the river, he moaned, when they could do it more easily at home? His promise to his Dream Girl was a ridiculous one. She'd soon get used to fish heads. And the sooner he took them home, the sooner she'd get used to them. That very afternoon he ordered his servant to take his catch home whole. The boy paled and started shaking when his master made his command. 'But sir,' the boy protested, his eyes wide with terror. 'You know your wife's wish. I would rather run away than risk her wrath.'

'Fine!' shouted Masoka. 'Then run!'

That night, Masoka went home without one servant – and the fish heads still on. With the next day's catch, he commanded his second servant to do the same. That servant, too, refused, and the next, and the next, until on the ninth day, Masoka had only one servant left. 'I command you,' he shouted to the boy at the river, 'take the fish home!'

This time, though, the boy took such fright that he ran all the way home – with the whole fishes – to warn his beloved mistress. By the time Masoka had arrived back, not only had his servant vanished, but everything he loved: his beautiful home, his carved ebony furniture, his cupboard full of food – and his beloved dream girl. All that was left was his old mat under a tree.

Masoka fell on his knees, and wept, and prayed to God, promising that he would never ever bring home fish heads again. But it was too late: he had broken his promise.

And as Masoka had learnt, once one breaks a promise, something precious is lost forever.

The finger tree

Told to me in Ndebele by Justice Chinamhora in Harare, Zimbabwe

There was once a father who had only one son. He was very proud of his son, and had brought him up to be honest, brave and kind. One day the father became very ill. As he lay on his deathbed, he called out. 'My beloved son,' he said. 'I want you to make me three promises before I die. If you keep them, you will be happy for ever.'

His son nodded respectfully, promising his father he would do whatever he asked. 'First you must promise never to talk about other people's business,' the father said. 'Then you must never reveal to your wife the secrets of your heart. And finally, when I am dead, you must cut off my index finger and bury it near your hut. But you must never tell anybody.' Then the father closed his eyes, and died.

The son was an obedient boy, and before his father was buried, he cut off his index finger, and put it in a hole near his hut. At first nothing happened above the hole. But soon, after the great rains, a beautiful tree grew. It was the most magnificent specimen anybody had ever seen. Its trunk was the size of an elephant's body. Its branches were big enough to seat ten leopards. Its sap was so sugary it made sunbirds sing. And its flowers were so sweetly scented that girls would beg their lovers for a gift of just one red bloom.

Villagers came from all over the land to see the marvellous tree. Everyone wanted to know where he had got it, but the boy, remembering his promise, never revealed the secret.

As the tree became more famous, visitor after visitor arrived, many with gifts for the boy. People offered him cows in return for the secret, and cloth, and gold, but still the boy kept his pledge.

In the next village lived a cunning man who was jealous of the son's fortune. He wanted the tree more than anything in the world, so he too could be brought gifts of cloth and cows and gold. He tried growing a seed, but it shrivelled. He tried planting a stolen branch, but it died. There must be another way, he thought, trying desperately to think of a plot.

One day the greedy man had an idea. He told his most beautiful daughter to pack her bags and go to the boy's village with permission to be his wife. When she was there, he said, she should use her wiliest charms to win the secret of the tree. She was not to return until she knew it.

When the girl arrived at the village, the boy was so bewitched by her beauty that he happily agreed to marry her. As soon as the wedding was over, the girl did as her father had instructed, and set about winning her husband's heart. She cooked his favourite meal of goat stew and maize, and made him the finest beer. She kneaded his sore feet after a long day's work and carried cool river water to the fields for him to drink. But no matter how strong her feminine wiles, she never managed to obtain the secret.

A year after the marriage, the couple had a baby son. The husband was delighted and went to great trouble to show his wife his affection. He procured special treats for her to eat and arranged a great celebratory feast. He found the best nursemaid in the land to help her and wrapped the baby in the finest cloth. And he showered his wife with love and attention. He had never, ever been so happy.

After the great feast, the wife thought she would try again to learn the secret. 'My brave warrior,' she said to her husband, fluttering her big brown eyes at him. 'I know you love me dearly, and want to make me happy. But if you want me to be the happiest woman in the world, tell me just one thing.'

'What is that?' said her happy husband. 'What is the name of our beautiful tree, and how did it grow?' she asked again.

The husband loved his wife so much that he felt he couldn't hide the secret from her any longer. 'Your heart is my heart,' he said, 'so I will tell you. But you must promise to tell no one else – not even your mother and father.' His wife promised, and so he told her. 'The name of the tree is Finger of My Father,' he said, 'and it grew out of the trust of our hearts.'

That night, while her husband was sleeping, the wife packed her belongings into a bundle, picked up her sleeping baby and crept out of the village to journey to the house of her father.

The father was delighted with her discovery, and by morning he had spread the news around the entire village. 'Finger of My Father, the tree is called,' he trumpeted self-importantly. 'Finger of My Father.'

While the girl's father was celebrating his discovery, her husband was waking up to find his wife and his baby gone. 'My beautiful wife,' he cried, 'and my precious son! Why, Gods, are you punishing me?' When he heard the villagers outside shouting 'Finger of My Father', he knew at once. He had broken the most important pledge a man can make – that to his father and mother – and was now being punished. He knew that he had not only lost his family, but that he had to leave his village. His ancestors' spirits would ensure that, if he stayed in his father's village, he would have bad luck for ever.

Sadly, he packed a small bundle of clothes and food, took his hunting stick and spear, and walked out into the valley to live a life alone. The Finger of My Father tree never flowered again. It still grows, green and tall, its flowerless branches acting as a reminder of the power of broken promises.

Old African proverb:

'He who marries only a beauty marries trouble.'

The day tails were given out

Told to me in Xhosa by Mabutinki Mafatshe near Rustenberg, South Africa

Long, long ago, when the earth was still young, Lion was the only animal that had a tail. 'But then I am the king,' he reasoned, flicking flies off his body with his long, muscly tail, 'so if anyone should have a tail, it's the royal me.'

As the summer wore on, Lion began to notice how infuriated the flies made all the other animals. Swarms of the little black insects buzzed and they bit, and they flew and they nipped, but none of the animals had anything to whisk the flies away.

Lion eventually began to feel sorry for them. 'As the king, I think it's time I helped my subjects by giving them tails,' he decided. 'I won't give anyone a tail as long as mine, of course, because only the king should have such a magnificent specimen. But I will give each of them something that will help them to flick away those pesky flies.'

That morning he started to make all sorts of tails – long and short, thin and fat, spiky and bushy, and round and stubby, spotted and striped. By midday, he'd fashioned all sorts of attachments, and hung them in a row on a long branch so he could admire them.

After he had decided which tail to give to which animal, he summoned one of his trusty messengers, Baboon. 'I have decided to give all the animals a gift,' he said to the rosy-bottomed creature. 'Please go and tell them I wish to see them tomorrow morning. Every single animal must come, as I have a gift for each of them.'

The baboon, delighted at being given such an important task, was soon jumping from rock to rock and tree to tree, running through grass and over rivers, relaying the royal message. He told Elephant and Hippo, Kudu, Eland and Impala, Antbear and Monkey – every animal from the largest to the smallest. 'And every animal must come,' said the baboon, 'because our king has made each one of us a special present.'

The animals were all very excited, for it wasn't often the king gave away gifts. Only the fat, furry dassies, were not bothered – they are lazy animals who would rather lie in the sun on a rock than walk into the valley to see the king. So they thanked Baboon, then dozed off again on their warm rocks.

The next morning, the valley streamed with excited creatures, on their way to get their gifts. Only the dassies lay about on their rocks. 'Aren't you coming, dassies?' shouted the troops of monkeys, as they chattered past. 'The king will be very cross if you don't!'

The father dassie rolled over on his tummy and looked at them through half-closed eyes. 'No,' he said lazily, enjoying the warm rock on his belly. 'I'm sure he won't have anything for such small and insignificant creatures as us. If he does, though, would you mind bringing it back for us?'

The monkeys reluctantly agreed, and went on their way, swinging and screeching through the trees into the valley. When they got to Lion's royal rock, there was their king, proudly surveying a branch on which he'd hung of all sorts of tails. There were dotted ones and striped ones, long ones and short ones, stubby ones and fluffy ones, straight ones and whirly ones. They were all sorts of colours, too – red and striped, or yellow and dotted, or black and white. What a fantastic array!

The animals roared and chattered and screeched with excitement, each trying to guess which tail they'd get. 'Silence!' roared the king, getting flustered, 'or you will make me forget which one I made for each of you.' The king, you see, was getting a bit old and his memory was fading. He picked up the first tail on the branch – a tiny one with sharp black bristles – and then called out. 'Right, Antbear, I think I made this for you. Oh, actually, no that's a mistake. I think it's for Monkey. No, I mean, um, oh dear, I can't remember! Oh yes! It was for Hippo! Come Hippo, come and collect your tail!'

While Hippo was very pleased that he'd been the first animal to be given his tail, he was not very pleased about its size. What was a great big animal like him going to do with such a tiny tail? It wouldn't do at all do have such a stubby specimen! But he couldn't complain, so graciously he let the king attach it to his bottom and then showed it off to the other animals.

The next tail on the branch was a great brown bushy creation that fluffed out at the sides and waved about in the air. It was so beautiful

that all the animals wanted it. But once again the king paused. 'Now who did I make this for?' he said, scratching his head absentmindedly. 'Was it for Giraffe? Or for Rhino? Oh gosh, I can't remember. Well, it is brown, so I guess it must be for a brown animal. I know! Squirrel! Come forward Squirrel!' And so the surprised squirrel bounded forward for his magnificent tail, which he then flicked backwards and forwards with pleasure, showing it off to all the other envious creatures.

The tail-giving went on all afternoon, until at the end of the day, every single animal had a tail. But still there was one left hanging in the tree. 'Now this one I remember specifically making,' said the king. 'I made it for Dassie. Step forward Dassie!'

No one stepped forward, and animals were silent. 'Dassie, step forward please!' roared the Lion again. But still no one moved. Then Monkey edged forward slowly. 'Excuse me King,' he said, holding his new long black tail over his arm. 'But Dassie was busy sunbathing this morning. So he asked me if I would collect his tail for him.'

The king was furious. He had spent a long time making the tail for Dassie, but the rotten little rock rabbit hadn't even bothered to come. Still, it would be silly to let that tail go to waste, so he handed it to Monkey and sent everyone home. Soon the valley was full of happy, chattering animals, waving and admiring their handsome new bottoms as they wandered off into the sunlight.

As he had promised the king, Monkey carried Dassie's tail carefully over his arm. But as he got nearer Dassie's rock, he began to look at it enviously. 'Why should lazy Dassie get a tail at all if he couldn't be bothered to collect it himself?' he said to himself. 'It is such a fine long tail and if I added it to mine, I would have the longest in the kingdom. Even longer than Lion's!'

So the naughty monkey took the end of Dassie's tail and stuck it on to the end of his own. The combination of his own long black tail and Dassie's little white fluffy blob on the end made Monkey's tail the finest the kingdom had ever seen.

Dassie of course never got a tail at all – something he's enormously embarrassed about. Even today, if you spot him, he will lower his bottom and hide with shame behind a rock.

But its laziness is still remembered today. You will still hear the Xhosa people say: 'I-mbila yaswel' umsila ngoku-yaleza' which means 'If you act like a dassie, you will get the rewards of a dassie'. Which, as poor Dassie learnt, means no reward at all.

According to the Shona storytellers of Zimbabwe, the week after Lion gave out tails he gave out nipples too. All the animals gathered round the baobab tree to be given tips for their breasts. But Hen couldn't be bothered to go; she was too busy scratching for corn. So her friend Dog agreed to collect them for her. On her way home, Dog had a crafty plan. 'If I had extra nipples, I could feed all my puppies at once,' she thought. So, instead of delivering Hen's nipples to the chicken kraal, she attached them to her own body – one line of nipples along the left side, and one line on the right. She was very pleased, for ever since she has been able to feed six puppies all at once. Hen, though, has no nipples. The next time you see a chicken's breast, have a look. Can you see any?

The day Monkey saved his heart

Told to me in Bemba by Godfrey Chanda, a subsistence farmer, near the Kalamazi rose farm, outside Lusaka, Zambia

When Man came to live on the earth, God put him in a beautiful valley. The valley had clear rivers to drink from, tall trees to rest under, strong grass to thatch his huts and bountiful rain for his crops. Man loved his home.

In those days, Man had never seen an animal and the animals had never seen a man. God had separated them – animals on one side of the lagoon, and Man on the other. Man could hear the lions roaring, the hippos Hmmmmmhmmmmhmmming, the hyenas cackling and the baboons howling on one side of the lake. And the animals could hear Man singing and drumming from his side. But neither had ever met.

One day the animals' curiosity got the better of them, so they held a meeting to decide how they should go about meeting their neighbours. 'Firstly, we need to see who they are,' said King Lion at the meeting. 'Then, secondly, we need to find out what that delicious smell is that wafts across the valley. If we knew what it was, perhaps we could have it too.'

The animals agreed. But no one could agree whom to send to meet Man. The small animals were too scared to go. The buck couldn't swim to the other side. Rhino was too bad-tempered to meet anyone. Giraffe was too tall to swim all that way. And Lion was too fierce. So Monkey volunteered.

'Don't be silly, Monkey,' said Elephant. 'You are far too naughty.' But then the king spoke. 'Yes,' he said, 'Monkey is naughty and can be very noisy. But who else has the skills that Monkey has? He can run on land. He can swing in trees. He can swim in water. He's got the brains to escape if he needed to. I think that's a very good idea – Monkey, you are the one.'

Monkey was very excited at being chosen by the king, and after he had waved all the animals goodbye, he started the long swim across the lagoon to the area where Man lived. He swam and he swam and he swam, his long tail trailing behind him. When he eventually pulled himself up on to Man's land, he couldn't believe his eyes. Instead of a jungle, there, in front of him, were huge areas of flat land, planted in rows with plants. Instead of trees to live in, there were little round shelters covered with thatch. And instead of an assortment of furry creatures walking around – like where he came from in the jungle – there were strange, upright, furless creatures who carried shiny tools about.

Monkey didn't like the look of them at all. So, instead of introducing himself to Man, he quietly climbed a tree where he sat all day and watched what Man did. He saw him hoeing and ploughing, making fires and cooking, and washing and sweeping. Then, in the afternoon, he watched Man going into the rows and rows of plants and picking off them long green vegetables that smelt sweet and ripe. 'That was the smell that had wafted across the water!' Monkey thought excitedly. 'I will have to take one back for the king.'

That evening, when the men gathered in a circle round a fire, Monkey climbed from his tree and crept quietly into the field where he'd seen the men picking. The smell was like nothing he had ever smelt before – a mixture of butterfruit, and marulas and guavas and cabbage all rolled into one. Looking round to make sure no one was watching, Monkey pinched one. Hiding in the stalks, he peeled off its green layers and slowly started to nibble. The thing was delicious! So he had another. And another. And another, until his stomach was as round as a melon. 'I think it's time to go home now,' he thought, satisfied at his feast. He packed two into his little bag, and happily sauntered back to the lake to swim home.

Imagine his horror when from behind a bush jumped a man with a net which he placed over Monkey's neck. 'Screeeeeeeech! Screeeeeeech!' screamed Monkey in terror. 'Please let me go. I was sent by the king and I must return. Do not harm me, please!'

The man was not convinced, though. 'Sorry, but in our culture if someone steals from us, we take his heart away,' the man said. 'And while I have never seen a creature like you, you have stolen from us, and I must take your heart. Please give it to me.'

Monkey had never heard of this custom, but, as King Lion had said, he was a fast thinker in times of trouble. 'Oh Clever Man, Oh Kind Man, Oh Generous Man,' he said craftily. 'I am from the animal kingdom and we do not keep our hearts in our bodies. Our king keeps them for us. I agree that I have done wrong to you, and that I should give you my heart. So please will you row me across the river to my king.'

The man did not know what to do. He had never heard of a king keeping hearts before. But then again, he had never met a creature with fur on. So he agreed and soon he and Monkey were in his boat, rowing across the water towards the jungle.

Once they got near the jungle shore, Monkey started singing a song. The man couldn't speak his language, so he couldn't understand it when Monkey sang: 'Crocodiles, crocodiles, come out and greet me, or else this man is going to eat me!' One crocodile appeared. Again Monkey sang it. Another crocodile appeared. Monkey sang and sang and sang until the boat was completely surrounded by hungry crocodiles, forming a bridge between him and the land.

Monkey then jumped out of the boat and jumped across his friends' backs into the jungle. 'Foolish man!' he shouted. 'Do you not know that animals' hearts are in the same place as yours, and feel pain as strongly as you do? Know now that if you try to take our hearts, you will have to face all the animals in the jungle. We are all friends and you are our new enemy!'

And as he said it, the crocodiles all rose up out of the water and tossed the man into the air, and into their waiting mouths.

Man still hates monkeys for stealing his maize. And monkeys still remember their first meeting with Man. Today, if you see a monkey, watch what he does to his chest. He beats it with his fist in the very place his heart lives. It's a reminder to Man that animals have a heart, just like he does.

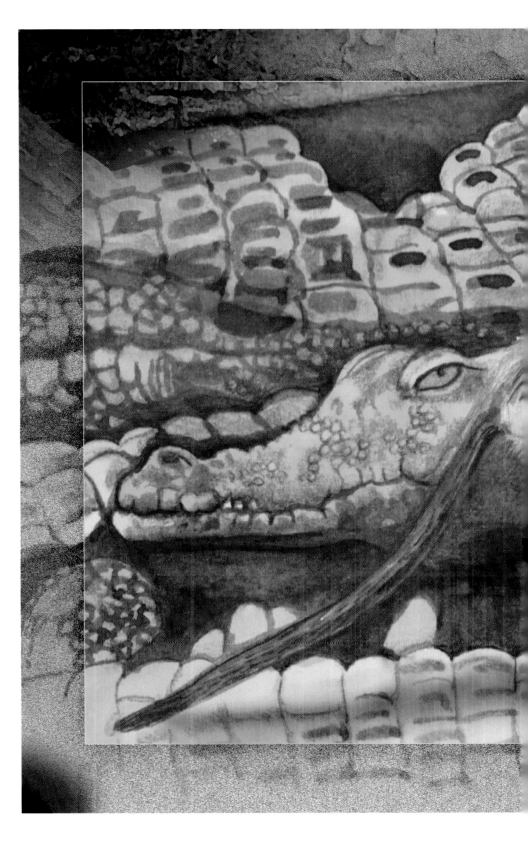

The day Man met fire

Told to me in San by Kgao Xishee in XaiXai, Botswana

Once upon a time, when the earth was still very young, Man had never seen fire. Everything he ate was raw – roots from the soil, milk from cows, eggs from birds, and fruits from the trees. All the heat he needed came from the sun – from its bright rays during the day, and the warm sand at night. And all the water he drank came from cool streams. Man wanted for nothing.

One day, when he was out hunting, Man looked up to the horizon and saw a tall, thin cloud spiralling up into the sky from the side of a mountain. He had never seen a cloud climbing from the ground before so, carrying his spear, he went to investigate.

Man got closer and closer, until at last he reached the mountain. There, on a stony ledge, he saw the cloud on the ground, cloaked in orange and red, and shooting out sparks and red trails. Man had never met a cloud like this, but, being a friendly man, he approached it with a smile. 'Hello stranger!' he said. 'I have lived here since the earth began, but we have never met before. Who are you?'

The fire was very pleased to have visitors, and urged the man to come closer. 'Please,' he said, 'warm your body on mine and enjoy my light. I am Fire, servant of the great creator of the sky, and am here to add pleasure to the world. Come closer, come closer.'

Man did as he was invited and was astonished that the nearer he got to his new friend, the warmer his body became. And the longer he stayed, the happier he felt. At the end of the visit, he was quite reluctant to leave. 'Please Fire, come and visit my home,' he begged. 'I would love my wife and family to feel the warmth of your company and the light of your face. Perhaps, if you liked them, you might even stay for ever.'

Fire had enjoyed Man's company immensely, but sadly said no. 'It is very kind of you, Man, but everything has its home, and mine is here,' he said. 'But please come and visit whenever you like.'

On that condition, Man left, and as soon as he was home he told his family about his new friend. 'You've never met anyone so beautiful,' he exclaimed. 'His feet were blue and purple, his legs and body swathed in red, and around his head darted flickering lights of yellow and gold. Even his breath, wife, was a sight: all clouds of blue and grey, with a crackling laugh. Oh, how I enjoyed meeting him!'

Again and again Man went to visit, every time begging his friend to return home with him. Eventually, his friend gave in. 'But please don't blame me if things go wrong,' Fire said to Man. 'I have an uncontrollable appetite and sometimes can't help eating everything in sight.'

Man happily agreed, and then set off home where he asked his wife to prepare the most sumptuous feast the village had ever seen. She cut fine fruits and dug up their favourite roots. She milked cows and sliced vegetables. And, as a special treat, Man gathered two ostrich eggs to drink. Fire had said he had an appetite, he thought proudly. But there was no way he would be able to eat all of this!

The day of the visit eventually came and on the horizon Man could see Fire leaving his mountain, his spire of smoke rising gently into the sky. At first, Fire was well-mannered and quiet. But as he got hungrier on his way down the mountain, his fingers began to flicker out greedily, snatching little mouthfuls of grass, then patches of dry bush. Soon he was eating everything in sight, his enormous flames pulling down trees and crisping the countryside. The friendly fire had turned into a big bad blaze.

Man wasn't sure what to do. At first, he enjoyed the sight of his friend's colourful body marching through the bush. Then, as birds and bushbuck started to flee past him, he began to worry. His friend had eaten huts, then trees, then the crops. What would happen when Fire got to him? He soon found out.

In a cloud of smoke and sparks, Fire arrived at Man's house and demanded food. 'I'm here, Man,' he roared, red arms flaming up into the sky. 'I'm hungry and I want to eat.' And from his body shot a great flash of light.

Man had never felt such heat, and with a scream, he and his wife ran from the fire until they got to the river. They jumped into the cool water and there they stayed, until at last Fire burnt himself out, and his great red body vanished in puffs of clouds. At last they were safe.

Sadly, Man and his wife wandered home. They had lost everything – their house, their fields and their crops. All that was left was a big black mess – and the black, burnt remains of the feast. But something else had happened in the house: the smell had changed. As they wandered from plate to plate, great wafts of perfumes they had never smelled before rose from the burning embers: crisp hot potatoes, boiled milk, roasted carrots and baked eggs.

They looked at each other in puzzlement. This wasn't what their food normally smelled like. So they picked it up, and nibbled. It was delicious. And it was warm and soft. 'You see, Wife!' said Man excitedly. 'Our friend may have ruined our house, but look what he has done to our food. It's a feast fit for a king!'

They called their neighbours, and from all around villagers flocked to taste the feast Fire had created. It was the tastiest food they had ever had. Soon, everybody wanted to invite Man's friend Fire into their kitchen – if he behaved.

With so many new friends begging him to return, Fire at last agreed. But this time he insisted that Man came to fetch him. As everyone had learnt, when Fire is left on his own, he has an unstoppable appetite. But if he is collected, and is surrounded by special stones that stop him wandering, he can be their best friend. He is warm. He brings light. And he improves good food. What more could a man need from a friend?

The day Hyena learned about luck

Told to me in Chichewa by Robert Temba outside Lusaka, Zambia

A long time ago, Hare, Lion and Hyena were friends. They ate together, they drank together and they hunted together. Every sunset they would sit by the waterhole, drinking and talking about the meaning of life.

One day, Hyena came to the waterhole with a puzzled face. 'Hare,' he said to his friend. 'I keeping hearing animals talking about lucky and unlucky, but I don't know what the words mean. Would you please tell me?'

Hare wasn't quite sure how to explain the words to Hyena. 'Just remember that lucky animals talk and unlucky ones don't,' he said. Hyena scratched his head. 'I still don't understand,' he said, looking downcast. 'Well, if you wait,' said Hare, sighing impatiently, 'maybe one day I will show you.'

Later that week, Hare met his other friend Lion for a drink. He noticed his friend was looking weak and thin. 'Are you all right, Lion?' asked Hare, concerned about his friend. 'Not really, Hare,' said the skinny lion. 'I am starving and haven't eaten for weeks. Look, you can even see my ribs.'

It was true. The lion's body was as thin as a snake's. Hare thought for a while, then came up with a plan. 'Meet me down at the riverbank at sunset,' Hare said, 'and together we will try and find supper.' Lion thanked him and, dreaming of food, he padded home.

Hare then went to visit Hyena. 'Your lucky day has arrived,' Hare said. 'Come with me and I'll show you what lucky really means.' Then he led Hyena down to a large tree on the riverbank and told him to climb it. 'But once you are up, don't move or make a sound,' he warned. 'Then you will understand what lucky means.' Hyena did as he was told, and soon all that was visible of him was his reflection in the river below.

Hare then settled down and waited for his friend Lion to arrive. Soon he saw the thin creature wandering up the riverbank. 'My friend Lion, I'm so glad you've come,' said Hare, bounding up to him. 'Look what I have seen for your supper.' He pointed to the river, and, sure enough, on the shiny flat surface of the water Lion could see a delicious fat-looking Hyena.

Lion couldn't believe his luck – supper, and so close, too! He sharpened his claws, focused his eyes, crouched down and, with a great roar, sprang onto the hyena on the river. But what a shock he got! Instead of delicious supper in his mouth, he got a throat full of water. 'Oh Hare,' Lion choked, coughing and spluttering as crawled out of the river, shaking water off his coat. 'I'm not sure what happened. One minute there was a hyena in front of me, and the next minute I was drowning, and now I am wet and cold, as well as hungry, so I think I should go home.' And off Lion padded, dripping down the path.

Hyena lay on the branch shaking with fear. He couldn't believe that his old friend Lion would ever try to eat him. 'Well, Hyena, you certainly know what lucky means now,' laughed Hare as the quivering creature climbed down the tree. 'You can still talk, can't you? That's a sure sign you are lucky.' Hyena nodded and, thinking about the lesson he learnt, he wandered home.

A few days later, though, Hyena had another query. 'Hare, I now know about lucky,' he said. 'But what about unlucky?' Hare was fed up with all this questioning. 'I have told you before: those that can talk are lucky and those who can't are unlucky. That's all,' he said crossly.

'Just be grateful you can talk.' But Hyena pestered him so much that eventually Hare gave in. 'Right, you want to see what unlucky is?' he said in a grumpy voice. 'Fine. Climb that same tree at sunset and I'll show you.'

When Lion and Hare met that evening for their daily drink, to Lion's amazement, he saw yet another fat hyena lying on the river surface. After his last experience, he was very reluctant to try catching the creature again, but he was still very hungry. So he took Hare's advice. 'The thing with life is that sometimes you are lucky and sometimes you are unlucky. Sometimes you have just got to look for the right signs,' he said.

Hare then stuck his second finger up into the air and pointed at the tree. Lion wasn't quite sure what Hare meant, but, as he'd been told to follow signs, he followed the finger and looked up. There, on a branch overlooking the river, he spotted Hyena. 'Dinner!' he roared, and leapt up the tree. Soon, after a bit of biting and fighting, he was munching and crunching, having the best supper he'd had in a long time.

The crafty Hare left Lion to his feast, and went home whistling down the path. 'I suppose it's a pity that Hyena learnt his lesson such a hard way,' he said to himself. 'But he didn't listen. I told him lucky creatures could talk and unlucky ones couldn't – so you would have thought he'd have understood the warning.'

Hyenas have been much wiser ever since. They are not friends with any one today – particularly crafty hares and hungry lions. Whenever you see them, watch the way they look at lions with suspicious eyes. They remember that day in hyena history when their ancestors learnt the meaning of unlucky – the hard way.

The hyena and the heron

Told to me in Shona by Miriam Mlambo,
who has been telling traditional stories on
Zimbabwean radio since 1956

Hyena has always been a lazy creature, living off the scraps from other animals' meals, but a long time ago, he didn't even want to do that. He wanted someone to look after him, to provide for him and feed him. 'What I need is a wife,' he thought, as he lay lazily under a tree, panting in the heat. 'She cannot be a hyena, for like me she will prefer lying in the shade. I need another kind of wife.'

One day, as he was walking through the forest to the river to get some water, he saw the most gorgeous bird he had ever seen. She was standing in a shallow pool, fishing, and as she dipped her head delicately into the water, Hyena noticed her soft grey wings, her delicate white feathers and her long golden legs.

'What a beauty!' Hyena thought excitedly, as he brushed off his dusty spotted coat and padded towards the pool. When he got there, he slunk forward and, with a sly smile, introduced himself to the bird. 'Good morning, beautiful stranger,' he said, his tail slinking to the ground. 'I am Hyena, King of the Jungle. Who, beautiful bird, are you?'

The heron was flattered that she, a simple bird, should be visited by a great king and her head feathers flushed with excitement. 'Why, I live here by the water, in a big nest with my family,' she said in a friendly voice. 'None of us has ever met a hyena before and I am sure my family would be delighted. Can I tempt you to visit?'

Hyena was delighted, for he knew that an invitation like that usually meant food. Being a greedy fellow, who enjoyed a good gorge, he accepted at once, and soon he and Heron were walking happily along the riverbank towards the heron family's great nest. As Hyena expected, the family laid on a great spread of fish and frogs and crabs and small birds – all freshly caught that morning. He had never had such a fine fresh feast.

Having thanked the family, that evening Hyena set off home and again began to think about a wife. 'Wouldn't it be a fine thing,' he thought, 'to be served such a fine feast every day? Perhaps I should marry the heron!' The more he thought about it, the more he liked the idea of being served. So the next day, after a quick wash in a jungle pool, he set off early to ask Heron's father for his daughter's hand in marriage.

Mr Heron was delighted. No heron had ever married an animal before – never mind a king – and he and Mrs Heron soon set about preparing a great feast for the wedding of their daughter.

The great day came and Hyena settled happily into the great heron family and being waited on by his dutiful wife. But one day she came to him. 'Husband, oh King, oh Lord of the Jungle,' she said dutifully, lowering her head before the lazy beast. 'The other male herons are going out fishing this afternoon and have asked you to go with them. Can I prepare a fishing sack for you?'

Hyena had never been fishing before, but not wanting to be outshone by the others, he grumpily agreed. When they got to the river, though, Hyena remembered why he had never been fishing before: he hated water and he couldn't swim. He had to find a way out of it. 'Brother Herons,' he said craftily. 'I know a pool where fish are plentiful, but can only be reached by those with legs. So I will have to leave you here. But I will see you later with my catch.' And off he slunk into the undergrowth.

Hyena headed toward a small, shallow pool along the river he'd seen. But once he got there, he stopped. How did one catch fish? he wondered. Besides, what did a live fish look like? He has never seen a live one in his life. Slowly, he walked to the edge of the pool, and careful not to fall in, he looked into the water.

There, in the cloudy green pond were all manner of moving creatures, leaping and hopping about. Some were fat, some thin, some high-jumpers, some long-jumpers. All were green. 'Marvellous,' thought Hyena, howling with laughter. 'This will take me no time!' He took his bag, scooped it into the water and soon had a sack full of wriggling creatures to take home.

Back at the clear pond, the Herons were having less luck. 'Well, that's why I am a king and you are not,' said Hyena with a smirk. 'See you later.' And off he slunk back to his wife's tree, under which he settled for a snooze.

At sunset, when the herons strutted back with their bags of fish, there was great excitement. Each bird lined up with his bag, and one by one, emptied the wriggling silver piles of fish onto the grass. Then came Hyena's turn. 'Of course, it took me only a few minutes,' he said arrogantly, and turned his bag upside down. When the contents fell out, the herons couldn't believe their eyes. On the ground lay a greasy, messy, wriggly, heaving mass of smelly green frogs.

The herons burst into howls of laughter. 'Kraaaaaaak! Krrraaaaaak!' they cackled, flapping their wings and snapping their beaks with mirth. 'You think those are fish, do you? Very funny, Hyena, very funny! Are you sure you are a king, Hyena? Wouldn't a king know these things?'

Then they turned to Hyena's wife, who was now blushing with shame. 'How on earth did you agree to marry this man?' they croaked. 'He doesn't even know a frog from a fish!' Knowing they were right, she hung her head. Her father, too, hung his head, realising he had been tricked into arranging such a ridiculous marriage. 'No wonder a bird has never married an animal,' he muttered. 'Those with feathers should stick together.'

Hyena, realising he had been found out, slunk off to live in hills far away, where he could hide. He's never tried fishing again. For even now, if he goes near water, you'll hear the herons mocking him. 'Kwaaak, kwaaak, caught a frog?' you'll hear them cry. If you ever wondered why hyenas slink around ashamedly, now you know why.

There are several variations on this story – one about a man who marries a meerkat (which steals all his eggs and chickens at night), another about a woman who marries a cow (which spends all day ploughing fields for no reason) and another about a woman who marries a dog (which spends all night scavenging rubbish in the dump until it is shot). They are told in every southern African country.

The day Hare lost his head

Told to me in Shona by Justice Chinamhora in Harare, Zimbabwe

In the days when the earth was young, Hare and Cockerel were good friends and lived opposite each other at the edge of the kraal. Cockerel and his wife Mrs Hen roosted on the roof of a hut from which Mr Cock crowed every morning to tell the creatures that dawn had broken. And Hare and his wife had a burrow nearby, which they had dug deep into the ground to keep their ten baby hares cool.

The two friends were seldom apart. When Hare hunted in the long grass, Cockerel trailed behind him, pecking up insects that his friend's legs had disturbed. At dusk, they would dip their heads down together at the river, sipping the cool water. And occasionally, Cock even shared with Hare some pieces of maize he'd found in the fields. Generally, though, it was Hare who was the boss, being the cleverest animal around.

One day, when Hare came to see his friend, Cock was doing what all cocks do when they rest: he was standing on one foot with his head under his wing. Hare had never visited Cock before when he was resting and was horrified. With eyes wide, he hopped round the hut, calling out to Cock's wife. 'Mrs Hen, Mrs Hen,' he shouted, his whiskers twitching with excitement. 'I went to see your good husband the Cock, but half of him was missing. His head has gone! And one of his legs!'

Mrs Hen was most amused that Hare was all a-twitch, because normally the vain creature knew everything. 'What Mr Hare?' said

Mrs Hen. 'Do you mean you can't do that? Obviously my husband is a much cleverer creature than you. When he fancies a rest, he just sends off his leg and his head to do his hunting for him while he stays behind at home in the shade. I'm surprised you don't do that, too, Mr Hare. Perhaps you aren't so clever after all.'

Hare didn't like being looked down on by a mere kraal chicken and would have liked to have given the clucky Mrs Hen a sharp kick with his back legs. But, being a crafty creature, he merely said: 'Of course I can do that old trick, Mrs Hen. I just hadn't realised that Cock could too. I would be delighted if, when Cock's head is back from hunting, you both came over to my house for a drink to witness my own ability to do the same.' With a haughty little kick, he leapt off into the air, and in a couple of bounds was home.

Back in his burrow, he immediately told Mrs Hare about his discovery. 'Do you know that, while Cock is resting in the shade, one leg and his head are out hunting for him?' said Mr Hare. Mrs Hare shook her floppy ears. 'Anyway, I have decided that when the pair of them come for a drink later, I will have to show him that I, too, can do the same. After all, I am the cleverest creature in the land. Prepare the beer, and get out the axe, Mrs Hare, for we are about to show Cock not to be so cheeky with me!'

The timid Mrs Hare couldn't believe her ears. 'I couldn't possibly chop off your head, my darling Hare,' she said. 'Who will look after our ten babies? Who will find me soft, nourishing roots to eat? And who will help me extend our beautiful burrow?' But Hare was adamant. 'Mrs Hare,' he said sternly, looking down his nose at his pretty little bunny wife. 'Am I not the cleverest animal in the kingdom? If Cock can cut off his head for a while, then why shouldn't I? Do as I say and cut my head off. Then when our guests arrive, greet them and feed them. When they are full, my head will be back from hunting.'

Sighing, Mrs Hare picked up the axe and with one big swipe, she chopped off his head. 'Now, off you go, head of Mr Hare,' she said.

'Get up and go hunting!' But Hare's head just lay there. 'Hunt, head of Mr Hare, hunt!' she ordered again, pointing her finger at her husband's head. Still it remained motionless on the floor.

Just then there was a knock at the door. When Mrs Hare went to open it, there stood the fine-feathered figures of Mr Cock and Mrs Hen, ready for their drink. Mrs Hare didn't know what to do, but, remembering her husband's orders, she ushered the guests outside, sat them down, poured them beer and offered them some fine corn to snack on.

After one beer, Hare's head was still not back. So she poured them another, then another, making excuse after excuse as to the whereabouts of her beloved husband. But eventually, she couldn't bear it any longer, and crying huge bunny tears, she led them into the burrow where the late Mr Hare lay beside his head.

For once Cock wasn't at all saucy and Hen didn't cluck at all. All they could do was to comfort the widowed Mrs Hare and explain how Cock rested his head naturally with his head beneath his wing, before sadly going home.

As Cock crowed out the next day, he told the animals of the tragedy: 'Wisdom doesn't come from the eye, but from the brain,' he said. 'If Hare had bothered to think, rather than just look, he might be here today. But sadly, he didn't use his head, so he lost it. Hopefully, you animals will not do that.'

The animals learned a valuable lesson that day, which they still remember: don't always believe what you see. Think first.

The curse of the chameleon

Told to me in Nyemba by John Zulu in the Luangwa Valley, Zambia

A long time ago, when the earth was young, the Great Spirit looked down and was pleased. The trees he had planted grew tall and lush, the rivers he had filled ran with fish big and small, and the men he had created were working hard in their fields. 'I think the humans deserve a reward,' he said. 'They have tended their crops, worked hard and lived peacefully together. I will send a message to make them happy.'

The great god rumbled his thunder, darkened his clouds and called out to the chameleon, who he often used as his messenger. 'Chameleon,' he thundered, 'I have a very important message for Man. Tell him that I am so pleased with him that he will never, ever die. He will live for ever.'

Chameleon was rather pleased at having been chosen to be the god's messenger. 'So, Man will never die,' he said, swaying self-importantly from side to side. 'Now there's a special message to take. Gosh, I am an indispensable fellow.'

As he ambled slowly from branch to branch, his scaly green eyes swivelling in their sockets, Chameleon chanced upon a whole crop of insects, his favourite food. 'With such a feast in front of my eyes, how can I resist?' he said, settling down to snack on a fat juicy insect. One, of course, wasn't enough, and before he knew it the afternoon had turned to night. 'Well, Man's waited so long, I'm sure another day's wait will not harm,' he said, rocking gently towards a branch and rolling back his eyes for a good night's sleep. 'Good night, green forest, Good night.'

While Chameleon was having a marvellous feast, the Great Spirit was getting increasingly cross. The men he'd seen tending their crops that morning were now drinking, letting their animals wander, and fighting with their neighbours – all things he'd forbidden them to do. 'I am mistaken,' rumbled the god. 'Man must die after all.'

Again the Great Spirit rumbled his thunder, darkened his clouds and called out to Lizard, another regular messenger. 'Lizard,' he thundered. 'I have a very important message for you. Tell Man I am very displeased with him. So displeased, in fact that I have decided that he will have to die after all. He will not live for ever.'

The little lizard, being a nervous fellow, immediately dashed off, thrilled that the great god had noticed him. 'What a terrible thing,' he said, whisking his tail in the air. 'I must hurry and warn Man.'

Within hours Lizard had leapt over logs, scuttled under stones and dashed along dusty paths to the village where Man lived, without stopping to eat or even have a drink. 'Man, oh Man,' he said, his little tongue flicking out dryly. 'I'm afraid I have terrible news. The Great Spirit is very displeased. He says because of your laziness and violence, rather than having everlasting life, you will die.'

Naturally, Man was very upset. But it was too late to be sorry. He had done wrong, and now it was time to pay. Great unhappiness set upon the village, and when Chameleon arrived, the air was thick with weeping and wailing. 'Oh, stop this crying and everyone gather round,' shouted Chameleon self-importantly. 'I am the official messenger of the Great Spirit and I have extremely important news.'

Slowly and self-importantly Chameleon told them his message. When he'd finished there were great songs of joy. 'We will not die after all,' the villagers sang, their drums ringing out in celebration. Then Lizard stepped forward. 'Excuse me, Mr Chameleon,' he stuttered nervously. 'But on which day were you given the message?'

Chameleon stepped from foot to foot, umming and aahing and nervously rolling his eyes. But when at last he told the truth – that in fact he had not just stopped for a feast of radiant bluebottles, buzzy mosquitoes and fat horseflies, but had stayed in the jungle for the night – the humans were furious. 'If you weren't so greedy,' they shouted, 'we would have lived for ever. It is because of you, fat Chameleon, that we will now die.'

Chameleon was so embarrassed he wanted to vanish into the background. He shook, he stuttered, and he puffed himself out in terror, but still Man stood there shouting at him. Eventually, the Great Spirit took pity and granted him the ability to the change colour of his skin to match his surroundings when he needed to. From that day on, he's been able to vanish at will. Man, though, will never forget the cursed creature and knows that, whenever he sees a chameleon, bad news is just around the corner.

The clever little lizard

Told to me in Ndebele by Emma Matshazi in Bulawayo, Zimbabwe

Once upon a time there lived a group of the greatest lizards ever known. These creatures were not just monstrous, but magnificent, with great, green slimy bodies, long purple fingers, forked pink tongues and tails so strong they could flick a cow into the water. If threatened, the creatures would gather together like a great army, shooting up terrifying folds of red skin around their necks, flicking their tongues and hissing like dragons. They were called the Inxou.

The Inxou lived on the banks of a large river. By day, they would lie on rocks, sunning their scaly bodies, while their babies splashed and played in the water. At night, they would curl up in a forest, close their yellow eyes and emit loud steamy snores as they slept. No matter how well they slept, though, they would always be on the alert for their deadly enemy, Man.

Man was terrified of the dragon-like Inxou. But he was also entranced by it, because it had magical healing powers that no other creature possessed. If a man got sick, eating the liver of an Inxou would make him better. If a woman's baby died, chewing the liver of an Inxou would take away her grief. Every witch doctor in the country wanted the liver of an Inxou for his medicine box. Very few were brave enough to catch one.

In a village near the river where the Inxou swam lived a man and his wife. One day the wife fell very ill, but no matter how hard the witch doctor threw his bones, summoned the spirits and stirred up a potion of herbs, she wouldn't get better. 'There is only one cure,' the witch doctor eventually pronounced. 'You must mix these herbs with the liver of an Inxou. Do that and your wife will get well.'

The man was very scared. He had heard terrible tales of the terrifying Inxou. But he loved his wife and wanted to save her. So that night he lay in bed and thought of a plan.

The next morning he went to visit a brave warrior who long ago had killed a ferocious Inxou himself. 'Please my friend may I borrow your Inxou skin?' he begged. 'If I look like an Inxou, and live with the Inxou, I might have a chance of catching an Inxou.' The warrior agreed and together they covered the man with the Inxou skin, tying the lizard's front legs to the man's hands, and its back legs to his feet. How ferocious he looked on all fours! 'Those dragons will never know it's a man!' the warrior laughed.

The next day, the man set off on his mission, disguised as a lizard, and carrying a bag of beans, which he knew the Inxou loved. At last he reached the river, and in a lizardy voice cried out: 'My friends, my friends! I have a treat, I have a treat! Come and join me for a feast!'

The lizards looked at him suspiciously, as they didn't recognise this strange Inxou. But he had the scales of an Inxou, and the legs of an Inxou. And he had their favourite treat of beans. So they welcomed him and were soon feasting on their new friend's gift.

One day, as the man was lying on a rock watching the grandmother, a baby Inxou began to stare at him suspiciously. As the baby looked at the man, it began to sing a song. 'What type of animal are you?' it sang, 'What kind of animal are you? With hands and head like a man, but the body of an Inxou?'

The man started to shake, worried the other lizards might hear, but no one took any notice but the baby's parents who told it to be quiet.

But the baby took no notice and this time started to sing more loudly: 'What type of animal are you? What type of animal are you? With hands and head like a man, but the body of an Inxou?'

Before the parents could look at him more closely, the man scuttled off into the forest on all fours. 'Oh no!' he thought as he waddled away. 'My disguise has been discovered. I am going to have to catch the grandmother tonight.'

At dusk, while the other lizards swam in the cooling river, the man laid his trap: a trail of beans from behind the grandmother's rock into the forest. Then, he hid behind a tree with his spear. Soon he saw the granny's nose sniffing the air. 'Mmmm, Mmmm, I smell a treat,' she hissed. 'I might go into the forest for something to eat.' And, flicking her pink tongue, she started to follow the bean trail into the forest.

It was a silly thing for the granny lizard to do. As she walked towards the tree, her tongue flicking up the beans, the man took his spear and thrust it into her. Then, before the others missed her, he picked her up and carried her to his home.

The village celebrated the capture of the terrifying Inxou with a great feast and celebration. And, as the witch doctor had promised, a mixture of herbs and the Inxou liver, saved the life of the man's wife.

But it was the last time Man caught an Inxou. From that day on, the lizards listen to their babies when they call out warnings. Should you see one on a rock, listen quietly to what they say. 'Quick, quick! Go and hide! There is a man in disguise, we can see with our eyes!' you will hear them singing in warning.

As the Inxou proved, young creatures are often the best guards. For even if someone is in a good disguise, youngsters often spot it with their fresh, young eyes.

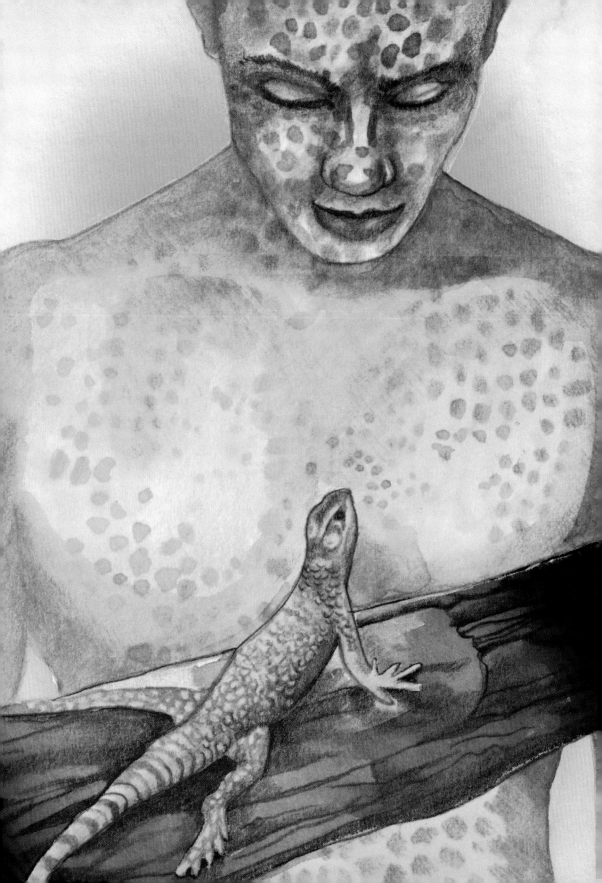

The charming Mr Hare

Told to me in Shona by seven-year-old
Grighton Hove, at Sebakwe Primary School, in
Zimbabwe, who was told the story by his granny

Once upon a time, when the animals roamed the earth freely, Hare
and Baboon were good friends. They loved eating maize (particularly
if they had pinched it from someone else's crop), drinking beer
(brewed by their loving wives) and playing practical tricks. More
than anything else, though, the pair loved pretty girls.

One day when they were walking to the river to get a drink, Hare and
Baboon spotted two girls getting water. Being experts at women-
watching, they quickly hopped behind a rock to spy. 'Look at those big
brown eyes,' whistled Hare quietly as he ogled the pretty creatures.
'And those glistening white teeth!' exclaimed Baboon, giving his own a
quick polish with his finger. 'Now they are what I call beauties! Come
on Hare!'

Brushing the grass off their fur, the two charmers strolled out of the
bush and strutted towards the girls. Soon, with their polite manners
and handsome looks, the pair had enticed the girls to share a sunset
drink by the river, where they giggled and fluttered their eyelashes.

As usual, the boys spent hours competing for attention. 'You have
never met such a great burrow digger as myself,' boasted Hare,
showing off his strong back leg muscles. 'If you need someone to dig
you an extra room, girls, I'm your man!'

Baboon gave a laugh. 'You may be able to dig down, Hare,' he said, 'but you can't climb like I can to the top of a tree to pick presents of mangoes, figs and papaya. If you want a boyfriend who will give you presents, girls, or a pair of nimble hands, I'm definitely your man!'

The boasting continued all evening, Hare and Baboon trying to outdo each other, until at last the time came for everyone to go home. As they were leaving, Hare took one of the girls aside. 'If you meet us in the same place tomorrow,' he whispered, 'you will see with your own eyes who is the greater of the two.' The girl nodded happily, and waved Hare and Baboon goodbye, shouting 'See you tomorrow' as they went.

The next day, Hare and Baboon got up early to spruce themselves up. They brushed their coats and groomed their tails. They flicked off fleas and picked off burrs. Finally, when they were ready, they gave each other a look-over. 'Very handsome, Baboon,' proclaimed Hare, giving his friend's coat a last minute dust. 'They'll love you.'

They set off but five minutes down the path Hare gave a groan and, holding his stomach in agony, fell to the ground. 'I'm ill, terribly ill,' whined the long-eared creature, wriggling and writhing on the path. 'I can't walk any longer, Baboon. You are going to have to carry me.'

Baboon had never seen his friend ill before, so, feeling sorry for him, he willingly leant down so Hare could climb on to his back.' Thank you,' said Hare, mounting Baboon with a sly smile. 'How kind, dear friend, how kind. Imagine how impressed the girls are going to be with your chivalry.' 'Indeed,' said Baboon, smiling happily at that thought, 'just imagine!'

A bit further along the path, Hare again let out another cry. 'Flipping flies! I wish they would stop biting me!' he said irritated. 'Would you be so kind, friend Baboon, to pass me a long leafy stick to swat them off?'

Keen to help his sick friend, Baboon amicably agreed, and soon Hare was happily sitting on his friend's back swatting flies with his long leafy stick. The peace didn't last long though. Just before the river,

Hare started screaming. 'Quick, Baboon, Lion is coming to eat us!' he screeched, clinging onto Baboon's back with all his might. 'Run!'

Believing every word, Baboon shot off towards the river, dust flying as his paws scuffled up the dirt. The closer to the girls they got, the louder Hare shouted, urging him on and beating him with his long new stick. 'Faster, Baboon, faster!' he screeched. 'If you don't get us to the river, we will be Lion's dinner!'

Baboon ran and ran and ran. When at last they reached the river, where the two girls were waiting, he was hot, dusty, sweaty and exhausted. Not Hare, though. 'Why, hello girls,' he said smoothly, hopping off his friend's back. 'Isn't it wonderful to have friend who will transport you about?'

The two girls smiled at Hare, captivated by his charisma. Imagine, they thought, having a boyfriend with his own transport! 'What a wonderful, handsome and clean creature you are, Mr Hare,' they cooed, as Baboon stood by, filthy and sweaty. 'Can we offer you a drink, my dear?'

And off they swayed, arm-in-arm with Mr Hare, towards the river for a drink, chatting and laughing and enjoying his wit and his charm.

Baboon, sitting exhausted in the dust, was humiliated and very, very cross. But realising that he had no chance of charming the girls with his muddy paws, dusty coat and sweaty face, he grumpily put his tail between his legs and swung off home through the trees, vowing to revenge his cheating chum.

Hare, being the charming chap he is, won the hearts of both women, and took them both home as wives. Even today look and see how many wives and girlfriends and children he has. It will definitely be more than one. He isn't called the Charming Chap of the Jungle for nothing.

The baboon's party

Told to me in Shona by Talent Tabengwa, a Methodist pastor in the Chiwundura communal area near Kwekwe, Zimbabwe

Once upon a time Hare and Baboon were close friends. Every morning, they would wake up, eat breakfast and walk to the fields to farm their crops. There Baboon pulled the plough to break up the soil and Hare hopped from one side to the other, planting seeds. They were a fine team.

One year their millet crop was so good that Baboon decided to have a party. He called his wife and asked her to prepare big barrels of beer, brewed from their millet. 'Yipppppeeeeee!' she screamed, jumping wildly from branch to branch. 'A party!' Then she swung off the branch to start brewing.

After a few weeks Mrs Baboon's beer was ready and the couple started to issue invitations. When it came to Hare's invitation, though, Mrs Baboon paused. 'I know you and Hare are good friends,' she said to her husband, 'but he has his own share of millet to brew beer from. I am not going to give him any of mine.' Mr Baboon, being rather scared of his sharp-toothed wife, agreed. But he was secretly worried. How was his wife going to keep a clever fellow like Hare away from a party?

Mrs Baboon, of course, had a plan, and when the day of the party came, she woke up early and started to carry the calabashes of beer up a very high tree. So that was how she was going to keep Hare away! Mr Baboon smiled. Hare couldn't climb!

The party was a great hit, and soon the jungle was filled with the sounds of Baboons screeching and yelling. When Hare heard the noise, he went to investigate. 'Hey friend Baboon!' he yelled from the ground, 'Can I come to your party?' Hearing the cry, Mrs Baboon climbed to a low branch to greet him. 'Of course Hare, come up,' she said, her long teeth glinting as she smiled. 'As I am sure you know, baboon beer has to be drunk up a tree, not on the ground. But please, come and join us.' And off she went.

But no matter how hard Hare tried, he just could not get up the tree. He couldn't jump high enough to grab a branch, and his paws were too soft and slippery to climb the trunk. Tired, and very upset at his friends' meanness, he went home and cried.

His tears didn't last long, though, for in his burrow that night, Hare came up with a plan for revenge. First thing next morning he instructed Mrs Hare to chill their best beer. Then quickly he hopped over to Baboon's tree, where he invited his friends to a party. 'But be sure to wash your hands, though,' he warned Baboon. 'Mrs Hare wants it to be a smart affair tomorrow with lots of clean new beer mugs. She would not be pleased if you dirtied them.' Baboon nodded happily, pleased to be invited, and waved as Hare hopped off home.

That night, Hare prepared his trap for the next day. First, once his family were asleep in their burrow, he snuck out and from a nearby village stole a little piece of burning log. Then, after setting the grass outside his burrow ablaze, he hopped happily back to bed, knowing that when he woke, the grass outside his burrow would be burnt black.

The next day, just as he had planned, Hare's friends all hopped through their underground burrows to his house for the party. The only person to arrive from the outside world was Baboon, who called politely from the burrow entrance. 'Why hello Baboon,' said Hare good-naturedly. 'You're looking wonderfully groomed and glossy. Um, pity about your dirty hands.'

Baboon looked down and blushed. Hare was right. Although Baboon's wife had de-flead and cleaned him beautifully, his hands and feet

were filthy – black and covered in soot. How could that have happened? Embarrassed, he backed out and quickly ran to the river to have a wash.

But no matter how many times he washed his feet and hands, every time he walked back into Hare's burrow, the same thing happened. And while Hare seemed sympathetic to his friend's dilemma, he had to be firm. 'I'm sorry, Baboon, but you know Mrs Hare's rules,' he said. 'No clean hands, no beer.'

Poor Baboon. Soon, it was too late. Hare's beer had all been drunk, his food finished, and his guests were hopping happily home to their burrows. And Baboon had had none of it.

'Isn't it strange, my friend,' said Hare, as he escorted Baboon back to his tree, 'that in the very week I fail to climb your tree for a beer, you come to my party and can't drink either? Doesn't the jungle deliver strange justice?'

That justice still exists today. Have you ever seen a hare up a tree? Or a baboon down a burrow? There you are.

The king of the birds

Told to me in Xhosa by Mabutinki Mafatshe in Rustenberg, South Africa

Once upon a time the birds decided to elect a king. 'The animals have a king, Man has a king, so we should have a king,' they said, gathering under the branches of the ancient baobab tree.

Once feathers had settled, the roosters had roosted, the flamingos had balanced themselves on one leg, and all the tiny jewel-coloured sunbirds had stopped chattering, the meeting began. The little black swallow was the first to speak up. 'I think Ostrich should be king,' it chirruped. 'Kings are strong and powerful, and Ostrich is by far the biggest.' There was a murmur of approval from all the birds.

But Ostrich shook his head. 'Thank you, kind Sparrow,' he said. 'While I am extremely honoured, I believe the king of the birds should be someone who can fly, and sadly ostriches cannot. It will be of no use to you having a king who cannot see his kingdom from the sky, will it?'

The birds nodded. He was right. So who should it be? 'I've got an idea,' said Ostrich. 'We should hold a competition, and the bird who can fly higher and for longer than anyone else should be crowned.'

There was so much dust and so many feathers flying that nobody noticed that Quelea had hidden himself among the feathers on Eagle's back. When Eagle soared higher than anyone else, so did the cunning little Quelea.

After hours of flapping and soaring, most birds were exhausted, and soon only Eagle was left flying. 'Get the crown ready,' he called grandly to all his prospective subjects on the ground. 'Your new king is about to land.'

The birds were very excited. 'Hail Eagle, King of the Birds,' they shrieked, squawked and sang in unison. 'Come down and be our king.'

Just then the birds heard a sound which appeared to come from above Eagle's wings. 'Ping! Ping!' it went. 'Ping! Ping!' Everyone looked up and, sure enough, flying above the mighty eagle was a little quelea. 'Look at me! Look at me!' it trilled. 'It is I, not Eagle, who has won. Prepare a nest for your new king!'

'Nonsense!' cried Eagle, his golden eyes flashing crossly. 'It is quite clear that Quelea has cheated, for he could never fly higher and for longer than me. You must crown me king.'

The birds didn't know what to do because they had told Eagle he was king, but Quelea had clearly flown higher. So they all huddled up for an emergency meeting. This time Ostrich was the first to speak. 'What's important, my friends the birds, is to find out whether Quelea cheated or not,' he said, fluffing his wing feathers importantly. 'If he did not, he should be king. If he did, he should be plucked as punishment.'

Being rather a dapper little fellow, Quelea didn't like the thought of having all his feathers plucked at all. So without delay he scuttled off down the tiniest mongoose burrow he could find, where he felt sure none of the other birds would be able to find him.

He was right. Not a single other bird could fit down the narrow passage – which made them all doubly furious. 'Oh well,' said Ostrich, snapping his beak crossly. 'It's quite clear he cheated, or he wouldn't be hiding from us. We can't waste any more time with this silly Quelea. Someone will have to set up watch outside so when he comes out, he is caught. In the meanwhile, the rest of us should decide who should be king.'

It was agreed that because Owl is such a big and heavy bird, he should keep watch. Quelea, the birds said, would never be able to escape past the sharp talons and piercing beak of Owl. So, Owl was positioned above the mongoose's hole while the other birds went off for their meeting.

From his hole, Quelea listened carefully to their plans. How on earth was he going to escape, he thought. Then he came up with a plan. He knew that Owl liked nothing more than a fat mouse to eat, so, from the soft clay in the mongoose hole, Quelea carefully made a lovely, soft grey clay mouse, which he pushed up slowly through the hole with a stick.

Owl couldn't believe his luck. As you know, he can't see very well during the day, but even he could make out that shape, and it was a delicious snack! He leapt on it, pecking it with his sharp beak, then sprang back in horror as the horrible, sticky, grey wet clay stuck to his beak, his eyes and his face. Owl hooted and howled, scraping and scratching as he pulled the sticky pieces off his face. And as he did so, Quelea escaped.

When Owl discovered Quelea was gone, he knew he would be in terrible trouble. 'What will I dooooooo? What will I doooooo? Twit-boohoo! Twit-boohoo!' he cried. Terrified of what the other birds might do, Owl breathed in, and crunched his wings together, then squeezed his fat, feathered body into the tiny mongoose hole to hide.

When the other birds came by later, they were in a terrible mood, as no one could make a decision as to who should be king. The atmosphere became even worse when they saw the half-eaten clay mouse outside the hole and no Quelea inside it. 'That stupid, greedy Owl is even more foolish than the cheating Quelea,' said the birds. 'He, too, will have to be plucked! Let's get him!'

As you know, birds come in many different shapes and sizes, and some species are better at pulling creatures from holes than others. To get Owl out, it was the big birds who were needed, with their long beaks and razor-sharp claws. Stork was the first to be asked to try. He stepped forward on his spindly pink legs, lowered his head and slowly inserted his long black beak into the mongoose hole.

What the birds had forgotten was that, while Owls see badly in the day, they can focus perfectly in the dark. And as the beak came towards him in the dark hole, Owl saw it and bit hard. With screeches and squawks, Stork leapt back out of the hole, blood pouring from down his long neck. So Hawk bravely volunteered to try – with the same results. Then scruffy Vulture got a sharp gash above his eye.

'Let's go home now,' said Vulture, rubbing his red, sore head with his scraggly wing. 'Tomorrow we will be fresher and can decide how to punish this vicious owl.' The other birds were glad to agree. It had been a long day and none of them wanted to be the next to be bitten by Owl. So off they flew home to their nests.

As soon as it was dark, Owl crept out of the hole and silently winged his way through the forest to find a secret tree hole of his own. He has lived there ever since, all by himself. The only time he comes out now is to try to catch a real mouse by moonlight, when you might hear his lonely call: 'Hoot-hoot! Hoot-hoot!'

The other birds still haven't decided who should be their leader. If you see a flock of them round a pond or up a tree today, perhaps that's what they are trying to do: elect a king.

How Bushpig got a flat nose

Told to me in English by Zambian game guide Aubrey Mbewe in the Luangwa Valley, Zambia, who was told it by his Zimbabwean grandmother

Once upon a time, when the earth was still young, the bushpig had a beautiful, long, elegant nose. He snuffled with it in the grasses, using it to sniff out the tastiest, sweetest fruit and roots in the forest, and to dig out the whitest, fattest ants on the anthill. It was a source of great pride.

One day, when he was on his way to the river for a morning drink and a cooling mud-bath, he spotted the lilac-breasted roller doing one of its magnificent air displays. The bird was a natural acrobat, flying up and up towards the sun, before shooting down like a stone. Then, just before the ground, he'd do a neat little flip, and land deftly on a branch, right beside his wife.

Roller was a bit of a show-off, but his performance was obviously a great source of pride to Mrs Roller. On his landing, she would coo ostentatiously, fluffing up her lilac feathers and puffing out her breast beside her magnificent aerobatic husband.

Bushpig was mesmerised by the sight. 'Oh, how I wish I could learn to fly like that,' he said. 'Imagine being able to see the earth from the sky! And just think how proud Mrs Bushpig would be! Perhaps she wouldn't wander off so much if I could do clever tricks like that.' And he gave a little sigh.

The great African hornbill was standing by, listening. 'You can do anything if you really want to, Bushpig,' he said. 'Would you give anything to fly?'

'Anything, oh anything!' snuffled Bushpig, little tears running down his face. 'No matter what I do, Mrs Bushpig ignores me, wandering off with our little babies. But if I could fly …'

Hornbill had an idea. 'If I gave you some feathers, and the bees gave you some wax, then perhaps you could,' he suggested. 'We'd just stick the feathers on with the wax and that would be that. Come on, it's worth a try.'

Once Hornbill had pulled out some of his feathers, the bees volunteered an old comb of their wax, and soon Bushpig and his stuck-on feathers were ready to fly. At first he just tried jumping from a high rock, flapping his little legs, and soaring gently down to earth. But once he'd tried that, his mind was set. 'I want to fly high, high in the sky!' he cried.

The animals, excited by the commotion, soon came out of the jungle to see what the fuss was. Even night creatures like the nightjar and elephant shrew were woken from their sleep. 'Bushpig can fly! Bushpig can fly!' the creatures cried, looking upwards. And sure enough, flying above the trees towards the clouds the animals saw the strangest sight – a fat, hairy, long-nosed creature covered in black and white feathers, soaring like a bird.

Bushpig was so excited that he flew for hours – over koppies, above the grasslands, along rivers and through herds of buffalo. He flew higher and higher, until at last he could see the midday sun right above him in the sky. It was perfect. Bliss. Until suddenly he felt a drip. Then heard a flutter. Felt another drip. And heard a second flutter. 'It's not raining,' he thought, floating through the air. 'And there aren't any other birds around. What can it be?'

As he looked down, his heart sank. For floating below him were several hornbill feathers – his hornbill feathers. And below them were hundreds of jungle animals, roaring and screeching and neighing and howling, 'You're melting, Bushpig, you're melting!'

They were right. As he got closer to the sun, his wax had melted into a soft yellow mush, and one by one his feathers were falling off. No matter how hard he tried to flap his legs it was too late. His wings had melted. Nose downwards, Bushpig plummeted towards the ground, feathers and wax flying off his body as he shot down.

As expected, Bushpig landed with a terrible crash – face first into the dusty red soil, with his bushy little tail sticking up straight into the air. You would have thought things were bad enough. But they got worse. Just as Bushpig crashed, the wind changed. And, as you know, when that happens, your expressions freeze as they are. Nightjar's grin was permanently stuck forever more onto his wide bill – you can still see it today. Elephant shrew's long nose froze even longer as he whistled his horrified 'Shrewwwwwwww!' at Bushpig's landing. And poor old Bushpig dug his face out of the ground to find he had the flattest nose anyone had ever seen.

Mrs Bushpig was so horrified at her husband's stupidity that now she spends even less time with him than she did before. Now if you see her, she'll probably be marching through the bush, her little piglets in tow, with poor old flat-nosed Mr Bushpig trailing a long way behind. He's probably still dreaming of the day he flew. And the time when he still had a lovely long nose.

How Lion got his roar

Told to me in Shona by Sabine Sinjere in Mabvuku, Zimbabwe

A long, long time ago, Lion had a small, soft voice. 'Miaaaow, miaaaow!' he would squeak as he padded through the long grass, hunting for his supper. 'Miaaaaow, miaaaow!'

The animals all thought it was terribly funny that His Majesty sounded like a mouse and made fun of him behind his back. 'More like King of the Squeaks than King of the Beasts!' they would giggle.

One day, when the animals were sniggering under a great fig tree, Hare staggered by, almost fainting with exhaustion. 'Water, water, please, friends,' he begged. 'I have been hopping for hours, trying to escape Lion. He's out hunting, and with his silly squeak, I didn't hear him coming.'

After giving Hare some water, the animals sat in a circle, chatting. Hare was right, they agreed. It was impossible to hear Lion hunting with his silly squeak. Every day one of them was caught for his supper. But what could they do about it?

Hare sat for a while, sipping water from a calabash. Then he grinned. 'I've got an idea!' he said, jumping up from the dusty ground. 'We will give Lion a loud voice as a present! Then all of us will be safe.

Listen out tomorrow, friends!' And off he hopped.

The next day, as Hare had promised, he went to visit Lion. 'Your Majesty, you are a good and just king. And to thank you, we animals would like to give you a gift,' he said, bowing nervously before the big cat. 'We have asked the gods to help us find a voice suitable for the king of the beasts and he has found one. It is called a Voice Like Thunder.'

The king was delighted. His subjects had never given him a gift before and he wasn't too sorry about losing his soft squeak. 'Why, thank you, Hare,' he said gratefully, holding out his royal paw expectantly. But Hare shook his head. 'I can't give it to you here, King,' he said. 'Your new voice is so precious that we have had to hide it in the forest. You will have to come and get it fitted there.'

The king agreed, and at lunchtime the pair met in the centre of the forest. There, Hare gave the king three instructions. 'First, so as not to spoil the surprise, you must close your eyes,' he said sternly. 'Secondly, you must open your mouth, so we can fit your new voice into your throat. And thirdly, once your voice has been fitted, you must keep your mouth closed until sunset. New voices take a while to settle in and if you open up, it will escape. Got that?'

The king nodded solemnly and soon he was lying under a tree, eyes closed, mouth open, ready for delivery of his new voice. Hare grinned to himself. 'What a clever fellow I am!' he chuckled quietly, rubbing his paws together in glee.

Once Lion was settled, Hare set about collecting the king's voice. First he picked up a long stick, and poked it into a hole in the tree. Then he pulled out exactly what he'd hoped for on the end of his stick: a great big waxy honeycomb – and hundred and hundreds of angry bees. 'Just as I planned,' Hare thought as he lowered the honeycomb into Lion's open mouth. 'Now open up wide, your Majesty,' he instructed, with a grin. 'Then, please, once your voice is in, keep your mouth closed.'

For a while, Lion did as he was told. He rather enjoyed the taste of his new voice, he thought. It was as sweet as honey! After a while, though, it began to sting a bit. Then a lot. Soon it was throbbing with pain. He opened his eyes in terror, desperate to cry out. Then he saw Hare in front of him.

'Be a king, Your Majesty! Be brave!' Hare ordered. 'Remember, that when a Voice Like Thunder is born, it hurts. But we wouldn't want the animal kingdom to know that a little pain had made you give their gift away, would we?'

'Grrrrrrrrrrrrr!' Lion growled, his mouth clamped shut with agony. 'Grrrrrrr!' Throughout the afternoon, the Lion lay unhappily, his head on his paws, and great growls of pain reverberating through the jungle. At sunset Hare could see the king's patience was running thin. 'Well done, Your Majesty,' he said to the grumpy king. 'Your voice is nearly born. So, I'm going to get the rest of the animals to come and celebrate. Lie there for a while and we will be back.'

For another hour, the king lay in agony, moaning and growling. Then another hour. Soon the jungle was completely dark. But still Hare wasn't back. At last Hyena came along, looking for scraps of food. 'What are you doing, King?' he giggled, seeing the look on Lion's face. The king could bear the pain no longer and in agony he opened his mouth. Instead of his little squeak, though, out flew a great swarm of bees, buzzing and bombing and stinging with all their might. 'Rooooooooarrrrrrrr!' Lion howled in pain and anger, as bees stung his nose and eyes and ears and tail. 'Rooooooooarrrrrrrr!'

The animals, hearing the terrifying noise, realised Hare had done just as he'd promised. Quickly, they hid in every safe nook they could find: Aardvark down his anthole, Leopard up his tree, Baboon on to his rocky koppie, and Hare into the very depths of his burrow.

Even now, when they hear his roar, the animals quake and make their escape. For, as they know, the king is not just after Hare, who tricked him, but after every animal who gave him such a nasty gift. He has never forgotten that pain, either, and sometimes at night you can still hear him moaning and groaning, remembering the day he was given his Voice Like Thunder.

How Bat got his wings

Told to me in Zulu by Lindiwe Ndaba in Johannesburg, South Africa

Once upon a time, long ago in the African jungle, lived a mouse. This mouse was a great complainer, squeaking here and there about his misfortunes. No matter how good his life was, he would find something to moan about. 'I hate being small,' he'd complain to Elephant. 'If only I were as big as you, then no one would stand on me.' Or he'd gripe to Gnu about his squeaky voice. Sometimes he would even complain about his colour. 'If I weren't black, birds wouldn't be able to pick me out in the grass,' he grumbled.

One day, when he was in a particularly ratty mood, Mouse decided to beg a favour from King Lion. The king, everyone knew, could do anything. 'Please, oh gracious King, give me wings,' he begged. 'I can't stand my life any longer – with birds eating me, creatures standing on me and no one listening to my little squeaky voice.' The king looked puzzled. 'But you are a lovely, delicate little mouse,' he growled softly. 'You are not made to fly. Like me, or Elephant, or Antbear, or Eland, you were made to walk on the earth, not fly in the sky. Creatures that fly have feathers and beaks, not fur and tails like us. Now go away Mouse, and enjoy gifts you have been given.'

But Mouse, being a professional moaner, wasn't going to be pushed away that easily. 'King,' he protested in a squeak so squeaky it made Lion wince, 'I want wings. I neeeeeeeed wings. I am desperate for wings. Pleeeeeeeease give me wings to fly high in the sky!'

His squeak was so insistent and his manner so annoying that eventually the king gave in. But there was one condition attached to the gift. 'Take these wings and you will become a flying creature for ever,' Lion warned. 'Once you have taken to the sky, you can never return to earth again.' 'Yes, yes, yes, yes, yes!' squealed Mouse, leaping up and down on the path in excitement. 'Thanks for listening, King. Now if you don't mind I'll say goodbye. I've got to fly!'

Quickly he attached his new wings to his side, and with a great flap, he swooped off into the sky, his whiskers whisking backwards in the wind. For the first time in ages, Mouse had nothing to moan about as he fluttered and flapped happily, tumbling and turning, and swooping and swirling in the hot African air. He was so happy.

The only problem was that Mouse wasn't used to flying and after a few minutes, his wings began to ache. So, spotting a quiet, shady sicklebush tree, he flew down and was soon hanging comfortably from the branch. No sooner had he landed, though, than a thunderous squawking and screeching and squeaking erupted into the air as birds flapped in astonishment at this new furry flying creature. 'Who are you, you furry little creep? Where do you nest and what do you eat?' they squawked rudely, staring at him.

Mouse wasn't very pleased – after all, he thought he was rather a lovely looking fellow. 'I am a mouse and the King has given me wings,' he announced proudly. 'I have come to join you in the air, so I can escape everyone standing on me and trying to eat me. I don't have feathers or a beak and I don't make a nest or lay eggs, but I hope I can soon become one of you.'

The birds were horrified. 'We can't have an animal living with us,' Owl hooted. 'We have our own bird kingdom, with our own rules and our own king. I'm afraid you can't stay here. We're pleased you want to copy us, and fly like us, but you are going to have to face it: you are not one of us. Now off you go. Goodbye!'

Mouse was very upset, but with all of those angry looking birds around him, he thought he'd better make a move earthwards. So down he flew, back to the animal kingdom.

When he got to the king, he burst into a flurry of little mousy tears, but this time not even his high-pitched squeaks and squeals moved the king. 'I told you, Mouse, that if you took wings and took to the sky, you could never return to earth,' he growled angrily. 'Now off you go. I don't want to hear another squeak from you.'

Given the sharpness of Lion's claws and teeth, and the hungry glint in his eyes, Mouse didn't like to argue. So, sadly, he fluttered off to find a new home. But as Owl had warned him, he was from a different kingdom and not welcome in the air. If he swooped over a mountain, eagles and hawks would attack him with their long claws. If he roosted by a river, kingfishers and cormorants would spear him with their sharp beaks. And if he went anywhere near a tree or a nest, flocks of screeching, flying feathers would descend on him to chase him away.

'It's just not fair,' moaned Mouse, flapping his wings wearily. 'No one wants me. Where I am I going to go?' As he looked down, suddenly he spotted a cave – the kind of cave that birds hated. It was dark. It was cool. It smelt a bit like his mouse hole. And if he made little mousy squeaks, the sound echoed round and round the cave, making him feel like there were lots of other friendly mice like him living there. 'This will be home,' he decided happily, after checking that no one else lived there. 'Now that I have wings my new name will be Bat. And this lovely place will be my bat cave.'

Bat has lived there ever since. To keep out of the birds' way, he goes out only at night, when most of them are asleep. His eyesight is not as good as it used to be when he was a mouse that found food by day. But he's still furry and still very, very squeaky. Listen out on a dark night and you will probably hear him complaining noisily about the day he left his friends behind for a lonesome life in a cave. You might even hear his warning: 'Sometimes when your wishes come true, they're perfect for someone else, but not for you.' Isn't he right?

How Giraffe got his long neck

Told to me in Nyanga by Million Daka at Kisani Camp in the Luangwa Valley, Zambia

When the earth was young, not all animals looked like they do today. Lion was the only creature that had a tail. Hippo, then, was very hairy. And Giraffe was as short as a warthog, with squat legs, tiny brown spots and a fat little neck.

Although Giraffe was odd-looking, he was extremely popular. Every animal loved him, for not only was he kind-hearted and generous, but he could sort out any problem. If Lion needed someone to break up an argument, he would call on Giraffe. If an old animal needed assistance, Giraffe stepped in. And if little children fell in the river, Giraffe fished them out. He was the jungle's best friend.

The problem was, though, that Giraffe trusted everyone – no matter how nasty, mean or wicked they were. 'The world is a wonderful place and animals are a beautiful race,' he'd say, blinking his long eyelashes dreamily. And off he'd trot to help the latest creature in distress – a stork stuck in the mud, a frog with a sore throat, or a monkey with a tangled tail.

One day, when lazy Crocodile started crying in his pond, there was only one animal who felt sorry for him: Giraffe. 'Leave the creep to weep,' all the other animals warned, eyeing Crocodile suspiciously. 'He'll beat you or unseat you, or may even eat you.' But Giraffe, being Giraffe, ignored them.

At the edge of Crocodile's pond he asked the crying creature what the matter was. 'Oh dear Giraffe,' said Crocodile, tears streaming down his long nose. 'I ate a fish and got a bone stuck in my throat. It's so painful and sore, I just want to roar!'

'Fibber,' muttered Frog. 'Trickster!' snorted Tortoise. 'Liar,' said Lion. But still Giraffe stepped further forward into the pond. The animals began to panic. 'Don't believe him! Don't believe him!' trumpeted Elephant on the riverbank. 'That clever crocodile may be crying, but he's probably cheating, tricking and lying!'

But Giraffe couldn't bear seeing Crocodile's tears any longer. So, he balanced on the edge of the green pond, put his neck out over the water and asked Crocodile to open his mouth wide.

Crocodile was delighted to do so. And just as Giraffe leaned forward, the hungry creature cracked down its jaws, biting down hard on Giraffe's neck. 'Quick, quick, give it stick!' trumpeted Elephant, grabbing onto Giraffe's legs with his trunk. 'Save him!' At once, all the animals took hold of Giraffe. As Crocodile heaved, they hauled. As he wrenched, they yanked, with Giraffe giving great cries as his body was pulled this way and that, stretching his legs, his skin, his neck, and even his spots. Eventually, though, the old fat Crocodile got too tired to hold on any longer, and with a cross 'Phoooooooarr!' he let go of Giraffe's neck and disappeared into the water in a mass of huffing bubbles.

For the first time in his life, Giraffe flew – right up into the air. Then he landed, with a thump, on a pile of roaring, groaning and moaning friends. As each animal got up, it stared in amazement at the stretched giraffe before it. Instead of a squat little creature, there stood the tallest, longest-necked animal anyone had ever seen. His legs reached the top of Elephant's head. His neck was as long as Ostrich's. And his tail trailed past his knobbly knees. He was one of the most beautiful creatures anyone had ever seen.

King Lion was the first to speak. 'Of all the animals in my kingdom, it is you who most deserves this beautiful new body,' he said, standing proudly beside his now tall friend. 'You have always had a beautiful heart inside, and now you have a beautiful skin too. You will be a reminder that good things come to those who deserve them.'

As for Crocodile, no animal will ever trust him again. He can cry all he likes in his deep, dark pool and no one will come near. For they know he is trying to trick them with his fake crocodile tears.